It was more than a place...

it was an experience involving the whole mind and body. Suddenly there I was in the light, everything that is me vibrating to some strange new quality of existence.

Then I saw Hai Tsu, a different "kind" of Hai Tsu. She was naked, and her body was like some denser *concentration* of light. It was almost incandescent, yet I could see through it. She was about ten paces ahead of me, but when she spoke it was like she was speaking from inside my head.

"A thousand pardons, my master, but you must not be here. Danger here. Go back."

Suddenly Valentinius appeared beside her —his body shooting light just like hers. "We must respect her imperatives, Ashton," he intoned.

"We must?"

"To be sure." Valentinius stretched out a hand to me. "Come, Ashton."

It was not a self-volitional movement—I simply obeyed. I stepped forward and took his hand...

HEART TO HEART

The Ashton Ford novels
BY DON PENDLETON

Ashes to Ashes
Eye to Eye
Mind to Mind
Life to Life
Heart to Heart
Time to Time*

Published by
POPULAR LIBRARY

forthcoming

DON PENDLETON

HEART TO HEART

AN ASHTON FORD NOVEL

POPULAR LIBRARY

An Imprint of Warner Books, Inc.

A Warner Communications Company

11-87

This is a work of fiction. Any similarity to actual persons, groups, organizations, or events is not intended and is entirely coincidental.

—dp

POPULAR LIBRARY EDITION

Popular Library® and the fanciful P design are registered trademarks of Warner Books, Inc.

Cover illustration by Franco Accornero

Popular Library books are published by
Warner Books, Inc.
666 Fifth Avenue
New York, N.Y. 10103

 A Warner Communications Company

Printed in the United States of America

First Printing: November, 1987

10 9 8 7 6 5 4 3 2 1

For my children and my children's children;
that they know me, and themselves.

AUTHOR'S NOTE

To My Readers:

Ashton Ford will come as something of a surprise to those of you who have been with me over the years. This is not the same type of fiction that established my success as a novelist; Ford is not a gutbuster and he is not trying to save the world from anything but its own confusion. There are no grenade launchers or rockets to solve his problems and he is more of a lover than a fighter.

Some have wondered why I was silent for so many years; some will now also wonder why I have returned in such altered form. The truth is that I had said all I had to say about that other aspect of life. I have grown, I hope, both as a person and as a writer, and I needed another vehicle to carry the creative quest. Ashton Ford is that vehicle. Through this character I attempt to understand more fully and to give better meaning to my perceptions of what is going on here on Planet Earth, and the greatest mystery of all the mysteries: the *why* of existence itself.

Through Ford I use everything I can reach in the total knowledge of mankind to elaborate this mystery and to arm my characters for the quest. I try to entertain myself with their adventures, hoping that what entertains me may also entertain others—so these books, like life itself, are not all grim purpose and trembling truths. They are fun to write; for some they will be fun to read. To each of those I dedicate the work, and I solicit their response. Please let me hear from you, care of Warner Books, 666 Fifth Avenue, New York, NY 10103. My warm best wishes to you all,

Don Pendleton

Love is the whole history of a woman's life;
It is but an episode in a man's.
                    —*Madame de Staël*

I wept and I believed.
                    —*François René de Chateaubriand*

This is the last of earth!
I am content.
                    —*John Quincy Adams* (last words)

FOREWORD

This is a story I never intended to tell, for various reasons. One reason is that it is basically a love story—which is not too bad in and of itself, but it is also a highly personal love story involving many tender depths of my own heart, depths that can be very painful to touch in retrospect.

The chief reason, though, is that it seemed doubtful until very recently that I would ever penetrate the perplexing mysteries of this story—and one must understand his own story if he intends to tell it intelligently.

Recent events, occurring long after I'd thought the story over and done, have focused my understanding of its phenomenal aspects. With that understanding came also the realization that this story must be shared with others. It's going to hurt here and there, in the sharing, but I now know that this is a story that must be told.

Turn the page.

I am about to meet an angel, I think.

And a soul mate, maybe.

But don't blame me if the going gets a bit wild from time to time. It is a wild story. Which is another reason why I never thought I'd tell it—but I give it to you now, straight from the heart. And I hope that you receive it in the same place.

My heart to yours then. And away we go.

ONE

The Summons

I didn't know where the guy came from. I just looked up, and there he was. I live on the beach, at Malibu. In California the beaches belong to the people. Private property lines end at the mean high-tide mark. So I get a lot of people walking by; sometimes, some very interesting people.

So maybe you forget to lock a door. And someone just wanders in. Wrong house, maybe. You don't want to act the ass, get all indignant, toss the guy out.

I was at the computer in my study, manipulating some data I'd developed at Big Sur. Pretty intense concentration, you know. But I felt this guy's presence. I looked up. There he stood, gazing at me from the open doorway into the living room. Total stranger. But I said, "Just a minute," and started the program execution before I left the computer.

He'd stepped back into the living room. The front wall

is all glass, sliding doors onto the beach, closed and locked. Main entry is at the opposite side of the house, rarely used, almost always locked. I checked it out later. It was locked.

So here stands a guy in my locked house. He's about forty years old, give or take a couple, apparently in vigorous good health, nice looking. Southern European—Italian maybe, or Spanish—dark, very well dressed by a European tailor, makes you think of blood lines, aristocratic lineage. You couldn't call his speech accented. Just the opposite, it was very precise but nicely flowing, not exactly Empire English and not exactly American English, just sort of . . . neutral.

"I hope you will pardon the intrusion," he says to me in that almost but not quite stiff manner of speaking.

I say, "It's okay. Who were you looking for?" I go to the glass door, unlock it, slide it open.

Meanwhile he is telling me, "I am not here by error, Ashton. You are the man for me."

I reply to that, "Has to work both ways. Maybe you are not the man for me."

This guy wears his hair in a curious, old-world fashion—almost like eighteenth century. It is jet black, full at the sides and back and sort of flipped up at the ends in soft waves. You can't see his ears. He has a thin mustache. Stands very erect, almost stiff; feet almost touching, hands behind the back.

He tells me, "Let me assure you that you shall enjoy the assignment. A very beautiful woman is involved. And, of course, the pay is good. I understand that your usual fee is five hundred dollars per day. I offer you this, for ten days' services maximum."

He produces his hands for my inspection. Each is holding a packet of currency, crisp new bills with bank bands marked at $5,000 per packet. He thrusts the money at me. I do not take it. Instead I tell him, "We need to define the job first."

"It defines itself," he says, and drops the money onto a table. "Laguna Beach. Her name is Francesca Amalie. You shall find her at Pointe House."

I move to the table and pick up the money to examine it. Looks like the real stuff, hundred dollar notes.

He is telling me, "You must go today. The crisis is now. Help her to resolve it. Ten days maximum, or all is lost."

I am still checking the money. I ask, without looking up, "What crisis? Who is Francesca Amalie? Who are you?"

The guy is not responding.

I look up.

The guy is not there. He is not on the porch, not on the beach, not surfing, not in the driveway nor speeding away in a car; the guy is nowhere.

But the money is there, and the money is real.

My name is Ashton Ford. I am a psychic investigator, counselor, semiscientist, semicop, semi lots of things. What I am not is a semifool, not usually.

So I downloaded my computer, climbed into my Maserati, and took off for Laguna Beach—roughly an hour and a half south, traffic willing.

A wise man does not, after all, defy the angels.

TWO

The Point

Laguna Beach is something of an anachronism in today's booming metropolitan sprawl that is Southern California. You get a sensing of that during the early approach when you realize that there are but two ways in—which is contrast enough with the rest of the region, where the cities are jumbled together like the patches on a quilt and you can move from one to the other at virtually any compass heading without realizing that you have done so.

This little beach town stands quietly remote from all that, sharing her borders with only the blue Pacific and the verdant hills of the coastal mountains. Approaching from Los Angeles, you leave the urban sprawl behind at Costa Mesa where you have the option of continuing on along the San Diego Freeway to the Laguna Hills and then angling via two-lane highway through the twisting canyons to the sea and entering the town through its backside, or you can take the shorter jump from Costa Mesa to the coast highway at Corona Del Mar and roller-coaster on down to Laguna Beach through several miles of seaside splendor, with an endless postcard view of crescent beaches, soaring cliffs, and the Pacific flinging itself onto house-size rocks far below. I usually opt for the latter approach because it makes me think of the Mediterranean coasts of Italy and France, the Riviera—and I guess that is the best way to describe this particular section of California, especially the Laguna area with its riotous flora, hillside homes, and sparkling beaches.

But there is a human flavor to Laguna Beach that is uniquely its own—and there is something else too: there is charm. Think of that. In Southern California. Charm. It's a resort area, sure. Teems with visitors throughout the year, depends on those visitors for its livelihood, but here is a town that has remained true to itself, and you pick up on that very quickly. There are no Hiltons here, no Sheratons or Holiday Inns or Ramadas. The hotels and motels are smallish, intimate, colorful. There are no McDonald's or Wendy's either; some casual dining, sure, sidewalk finger-foods and courtyard cafes, but there are also many fine restaurants and most are quite cheap, with graciousness the keynote whatever the scale. You'll never go hungry in this town.

With all that, the heart of Laguna Beach is her creative community. This is an art center, a craft center, a fashion center, a music center. Charm center, yeah. She's a town that knows herself and loves herself, and she's fighting like hell to be herself. The resident population stabilized some years back at about 18,000. But the big developers have been hungrily eyeing her flanks. They want to run freeways through her pristine hills and extend the urban sprawl to engulf this lovely little anachronism and bring her into the late twentieth-century reality of gridlock and greedlock. I have to bet with the money. By the time you are reading this, greed may have already won the battle and what I am telling you about Laguna could already be no more than a fond memory of things gone by.

I knew all that before I'd heard of Francesca Amalie or Pointe House. I'd been to Laguna many times, loved to prowl the art galleries and browse the funky little shops, take in some jazz, or just stand on the corner and watch the cars go by. Great car town—if you like cars, and I do. Rolls, Bentley, Excalibur, Ferrari, Maserati—I'm talking *cars*, as artform instead of mpg, and you'll see all the car art on any afternoon in Laguna Beach.

So, yeah, it was no great sacrifice for me to tear myself away from the affluent ghetto that is Malibu for a quick trek to the charm center of California. I was between cases anyway and getting restless with my research studies. So I was primed and ready for Laguna, even without an angel on the shoulder, and even before I met Francesca.

Think of Gina Lollobrigida at about twenty-five, give her Bergman's haunting eyes and Bacall's quick humor, MacLaine's introspective smile, Monroe's vulnerable sensuality. Package it with a unique feminine awareness, call the vision Francesca, and you've got her in sight as I did that afternoon at Pointe House.

It should have been called Pointe Mansion, and even that is understatement unless you think of a sprawling seaside estate perched atop the sheer rock face of a narrow promontory. The point juts out maybe two hundred yards into the Pacific at an elevation of several hundred feet. The house and grounds occupy the whole thing, which is about a hundred yards wide at the base and triangles out to a width of maybe twenty feet at the point. The main house is built at the extreme tip; part of it even hangs out over the cliff, and that part has glass walls on three sides for spectacular views. The whole thing is cleverly designed to fit the land, has many levels, and—I am told—thirty-four rooms.

The grounds look like a Japanese park—gardens everywhere, artificial stream with waterfalls and footbridges, exotic trees and flowering bushes, several acres of that. All in all quite a package, and I would not hazard a guess as to its fair market value. But I can tell you that beachfront property in this area can go as high as a million bucks for just an ordinary cottage-size lot.

The gates were open so I drove right in and followed a winding country lane through the gardens for what seemed a couple of minutes before I reached the house. A young Oriental woman in black silk pajamas who seemed to recognize the sound of my name greeted me at the door and graciously ushered me inside. She put me in a holding area and offered me tea, which I declined, then gracefully withdrew. The room was larger than my whole house at Malibu. The walls were paneled in teak I think, and the floor was something like marble tile with heavy Oriental carpets scattered about in an eye-pleasing arrangement. There were lots of flowers and tables and sofas, some statuary, heavily framed paintings tastefully displayed on the walls, a breathtaking view of Laguna Beach through the only window.

I was still interestedly checking it out when Francesca appeared. She wore an artist's smock over blue jeans; barefoot; dark hair pulled carelessly back in a loose ponytail—an expectant, quizzical smile.

I'd never put much stock in the idea of love at first sight. Lust, maybe; sure, many times, but this was different—a sort of quiet excitement wriggling up from somewhere deep in the mind, something bordering on recognition or remembrance, an almost déjà vu feeling coupled with a lifting of the heart.

I just stood there staring at her for a long moment, probably with a very stupid look on my face. She must have been feeling something too though, because her smile was frozen in place and she was staring right back at me. We stood like that for maybe half a minute and a room apart, then she caught her breath and laughed softly, came on into the room, told me in a very pleasantly modulated voice: "Forgive me for staring at you like that. I thought at first I knew you, and I was trying to place you."

I handed her a business card as I replied, "Guess we both made the same mistake."

She dropped the card into a pocket of the smock without looking at it. "I was told to expect you," she said quietly. "Please make yourself completely at home. Hai Tsu went on to double-check your suite. She will be back down in just a minute, and I'm sure she would be very happy to show you where everything is. My only request is that you do not disturb me while I am in my studio. I'm afraid I'm terribly behind in my work, and I'm trying to prepare for a show next week."

She was moving out, backpedaling as she spoke, but I was moving right with her. I said, "Uh, I think there's been some... I don't understand what... what the hell am I doing here?"

She gave me a blank look; replied, "Don't you know?"

I tried to mimic that look as I spread my hands and told her, "All I know is that I was virtually ordered to show up here with all possible haste."

She showed me a soft smile, touched the back of her neck with exploring fingers as she said, "Yes, that seems to be the way it works."

"The way what works?" I inquired.

"That's the way I got here."

"When was that?"

Her eyes searched me bare before she replied, "Nearly a year ago. Look, you get the run of the house, nobody bothers you, you come and go as you please, the staff takes care of all the work—what's to complain about? Just relax and enjoy it."

I was beginning to get the lay of it now. I asked her, "This isn't your place?"

She treated me again to that soft laughter. "*My* place? Last year at this time I was sharing a loft over a store with three other girls, and we were just barely paying the rent between us. I'm here the same way you're here probably, as the guest of a very generous man, and—"

"What's his name?"

She blinked at me. "Valentinius, I think. Or maybe it's

Medici; I've heard both but I don't know which is the family name."

I asked, "What do the servants call him?"

"Only Hai Tsu speaks English," she replied, now showing a bit of impatience with me. "She refers to him only as *Shen*, but I believe that is some kind of Oriental title of respect."

She was leaving me again. I walked along with her. "You've been living here as a guest for a year and you don't even know the guy's name?"

She said, "Look, either stay or go, makes no difference to me. But if you can't stand a little mystery then I advise you to go. You'll have to excuse me now. I really must get back to work."

I told her, "The question is not stay or go. The question is why I was asked to come here. He said something about a crisis. Know anything about that?"

We had entered the "point" room. It was obviously cantilevered out beyond the face of the cliff. The vaulted ceiling was about twenty feet high and the three outside walls were glass all the way. It was an artist's studio to end all studios. Apparently the lady both painted and sculpted. Canvases were stacked everywhere and there must have been twenty clay busts scattered about.

I think she was unhappy with me for going in there with her. She planted herself just inside the door and said, very quietly with studied control, "The only crisis I know anything about is my show next week. I have been trying a year for this show. I have two more canvases to complete and twenty to frame. So if you will excuse me, please."

But I had gone on inside, my attention compelled toward the busts. Twenty, yeah, I counted twenty—all just alike, every damned one an almost perfect likeness of my "angel."

I turned to the creator and asked, very quietly, "Valentinius?"

She said, "Lousy, huh. Just can't seem to capture it. This is all very new to me. I'd never worked with clay before I came here. Now it seems that's all I want to do. That's why I'm behind for my show."

I thought the sculptures were great.

And I'd already decided to stay a while.

THREE

Reception

Hai Tsu is a real China doll, tall and willowy, the very essence of Oriental grace and dignity—very pretty, with that rose-petal skin so very lightly tinted into the gold spectrum as seen just now and then among some Asians and fulfilling the yellow race description of all. She has a voice to match—soft and gentle, almost whispery—and her English is entirely understandable, though a bit broken. Her name is pronounced *Hi-zoo*—or that is as close as I can get—and her usual look is that which suggests a bursting inner excitement or exuberance being held in place by servile propriety. You get the idea that as soon as she disappears into her own quarters, she is going to burst out with song or laughter and do a couple of pirouettes about the room. Don't ask her age; I couldn't peg that within five years, or maybe even ten. I can only sum her up as a beautiful young woman with a terrific attitude.

She showed me to my suite and steered me around inside to point out the various amenities as though sharing some delicious secret with me. A small but extravagantly appointed sitting room held a couch and two easy chairs, wine cupboard and wet bar, modular entertainment center with television and stereo.

Another room of about the same size featured a wall of books, library table, comfortable chair, computer desk, and a Tandy that looked exactly like mine. Hai Tsu's eyes danced a jig as she pointed that out. "Is very good?" she inquired, those expressive eyes scanning my face for approval.

"Very good, yes," I agreed, not wishing to disappoint her, but wondering also why it mattered.

The bedroom had an ocean view via French doors that opened onto a little balcony, a king-size bed, and king-size chairs, king-size desk—the whole room was fit for a king. The bath featured a circular sunken tub with shower and whirlpool, also one of those jazzy new sauna cabinets and a massage table. I could have fitted my whole Malibu bedroom in there and still had room enough for a normal bathroom.

"Is very good?" Hai Tsu inquired.

"Is heaven," I assured her. "When did I die?"

She almost giggled but hid it behind delicate fingers as she gracefully withdrew and left me alone in the splendor.

I found the whole thing vaguely troubling.

It was as though ... you see I am a closet hedonist. I

mean I live a somewhat Spartan life-style. My beach house at Malibu is an ordinary bachelor's pad furnished in modern basic and decorated to match. The Maserati is my only luxury; everything else that forms my personal environment is simple and functional. I don't know why that is, because deep down I would love to wallow in pampered luxury—and this suite at Pointe House was like a secret dream come true, a fantasy fulfilled. This suite was the real me. I recognized that fact, and it bothered me—or I thought that was what was bothering me.

But I found a lot more bother during the next few minutes. For example, the full wardrobe that hung in the closet—shirts, slacks, blazers, suits—all my size and my style; a shoe caddy with a nice assortment of colors and styles for every occasion, in my size; drawers of underwear and socks, swim trunks, tennis shorts; anything and everything I could conceivably need or want to clothe myself, and as I would so do.

And that was only the beginning. All my favorite albums were racked beside the stereo. The magazines I habitually read were all there, in their latest editions. A paperback novel I had been reading lay on a bedside table. The wall of books in the study included all of my most cherished titles as well as several rare classical tomes I would have loved to own, if love or money could have bought them.

The bother approached critical mass when I sat down to examine the computer. It was a Tandy hard disk, same model as mine—which is not exactly mind-blowing since it is a very popular personal computer. But when I fired it up and consulted the system directory, it offered me the same selections that I'd programmed into my own computer, and a couple of those were of my own private invention. I ordered in my personal client directory, fed it the access codes, and the damn thing loaded it in. Now you see, a computer is not a magician; it performs only as it has been programmed to perform, and *this* computer had no right to that stuff—not unless someone had moved my computer from Malibu to Laguna and got it here ahead of me.

But this was not my computer. Identical, yes, except for the special peculiarities of wear that creep into every personal device. This computer was shiny new, never used, never abused. It was not mine, but it had the brains of mine.

So sure, I was bothered. Someone evidently knew me as I know myself, even my deeply hidden self. And that someone had also evidently gone to some pains to please that hidden self. But why?

I guess it was the why that bothered me most.

And I was definitely bothered. Yes, definitely for sure, as the valley girls would say. But it was only the beginning of bother.

If this is your first encounter with the wild and wacky world of Ashton Ford, I think it is time you were told a little something about my background and how it is that I find myself in these interesting situations.

First, I think you need to understand that the name *Ford* did not come to me from my father. I don't know who my father was; I doubt that anyone does—not even Mother, whose quiet humor found it fitting to name me after the automobile in which I was conceived, on the backseat, I trust. She was of the South Carolina Ashton line, with roots in prerevolutionary America and sparse but fruitful branches in each succeeding generation until my grandfather's time. He generated two daughters, then thoughtlessly died without providing a male heir to the name. Mother never married, nor did her sister. I don't know why she didn't just give me the family name at the rear instead of the front; at least it would have been an honest name and properly legal. Not that it matters; my name is really the least of my identity problems. I have received hints in recent years that there may have been some special circumstances attending my conception, but I will not go into that here.

I spent my early years in a sort of splendid isolation at the family estate on the Carolina coast. Never saw another child until I started school. But that was about the only form of deprivation. And I manufactured my own "playmates"—or so Mother used to say. I had a lot of imaginary friends but they were consistently adult the same as every other being in my experience, and our playtime was usually more educational than entertaining. They would come any time I wanted them—and sometimes even when I did not want them.

That is the kind of early childhood I had. Not at all lonely. Just different. And Mother was always warm and affectionate when she was around, which was most of the time during that period. I started day classes at a nearby military institute when I was six. There was an adjustment problem lasting through most of that first year. Just didn't know how to relate to other kids. But it worked itself out, and I always had my other friends at home to fall back on. Those other friends stayed with me in fact through those first four years at the institute, always at my beck and call. But then when I was ten I took up full-time residency at the institute, and Mother joined the jet set. That was a time when I needed my friends the most, but they abandoned me too at that point and came only infrequently in dreams.

I saw Mother infrequently too—a couple of times a year in the flesh for brief but always warm visits, once or twice a month in dreams. Funny thing, I always knew where she was and what was happening with her. I would get letters postmarked Zurich or Paris or Florence and every one was déjà vu; I knew the content before opening the envelope and each letter was mere confirmation of something already shared in a dream.

I went all the way through the institute like that, but all of it stopped, except the infrequent letters, at Annapolis. The naval academy was preordained for me, as an Ashton. There had never been so much as a mention of any alternative. All of the male Ashtons by whatever family name were born with an appointment to Annapolis tucked into their little belly buttons. I never questioned it. But I also had no particular passion for a naval career, never intended to pursue one beyond the obligatory active duty requirement following graduation.

I had a rough time at Annapolis, but not because of the institutionalization and discipline that bothers most cadets. I had grown up in that, learned to cope with it, even to enjoy it in most of its aspects. But I grew very lonely there. All of my childhood connections had been severed. I tried to look at it as a natural consequence of adulthood—and maybe I just was not prepared for adulthood. I felt abandoned.

There were other minor problems too. I think I freaked out the medical people there. They came at me four times during my plebe year with batteries of intelligence and psychological tests and never seemed content that they had me properly nailed. But the testing opened some doors for me, both during the following three years and afterward. Seemed as though they gave me any class I wanted and a variety of special War College postgraduate courses. I actually spent most of my navy time in a classroom. Finally wound up at the Pentagon, Office of Naval Intelligence, where I rode out the balance of my obligated service.

Since then I have just puttered about. I have this trust fund, you see, which takes care of the basics, and I have never seen much point to accumulating wealth of my own, so I am really free to pursue those things that interest me.

That is what I was doing at Laguna Beach. Or so I thought when I went there.

It had begun to occur to me though, during that first hour at Pointe House, that something or someone was pursuing me instead. I never really set out to become or to be a psychic investigator. I am not even all that certain that I have any particular psychic abilities of my own. I do not do things; things do me, and I do not control them. I usually try my best to keep them from controlling me. That is never difficult—or it had not been to this point in my life. I had never seen or experienced any psychical phenomena which, in retrospect, should be feared or even mistrusted.

But I very often did not understand that which was

being experienced—and even though I had been conditioned from childhood to accept a reality which most people clearly do not inhabit, I had always kept both feet planted firmly on planet Earth, and I was as subject to awe and fear as any human when magic is afoot.

Let me assure you that magic was clearly afoot at Pointe House. And all my small hairs knew it.

FOUR

Glimmer

The telephone began ringing in insistent little bursts while I was still puzzling over the amenities of my guest suite. I stared at the phone briefly—I guess wondering if the call was really for me—then scooped it up and gave it a shot. "Yeah, who'd you want?"

I did not recognize the responding male voice. "Mr. Ford?"

"Yes."

It was mildly apologetic. "I understand you've only just arrived. Hope I haven't caught you at an awkward time. But it's really important that I speak with you at the earliest possible moment. Would it be convenient for you to come down to the library right away?"

I presumed that the guy was not referring to the Laguna

Beach public library, but I wanted to be sure. I replied, "You mean the library here at Pointe House."

He sort of laughed as he told me, "Yes. Sorry. I assumed you realized that I am using the house phone."

I said, "Why should I think that? Everything else seems to have come straight from heaven."

The response was vaguely troubled. "What?"

I said. "Private joke. Who are you?"

"This is Jim Sloane."

"Uh huh."

"Oh I . . . I assumed you knew. My law firm represents Valentinius de Medici. I have the papers all ready for you. So could you . . .?"

I said, "Give me five minutes," and hung up.

But five hours or five days would not have been sufficient to prepare me for that meeting with Jim Sloane.

He's a guy of roughly my own age. Handsome, well set up, athletic—has a quick smile that starts fading before it's firmly in place, bright eyes, sharp mind. He started out with me though in that lawyerly manner—sizing me, psyching me, categorizing me. Which is okay. Lawyers are always engaged in some kind of mind game; it's the nature of their business. I was exposed to some international law studies, courtesy of Uncle Sam, and learned enough to respect the game if not always the players, and enough to know when I am being lawyered.

Sloane had his briefcase open on the library table. Several documents were spread out before him. We shook hands and sat down with the table between us.

"Could I see some identification?" he requested.

I said, "Trade you," and slid my wallet toward him.

He showed me one of those flash smiles as he produced a slim wallet and handed it across to me. I glanced at his driver's license and a state bar ID, then slid it back. He took a bit longer with mine, jotting some sort of legal record in a small notebook, taking verbal note of my Naval Reserve status as he studied the card.

"Subject to recall to active duty?" he wondered aloud.

I shrugged. "Only if the sky is falling, I hope."

The lawyer chuckled, returned my wallet and immediately passed over one of the documents; told me, "This is your power of attorney. I suggest you keep it in a secure place. Safe deposit box, preferably. I have a copy, so—"

I could have checked it out for myself but I was too busy checking the guy out, besides which I wanted to keep his thoughts channeled along a specific path, so I ignored the document and asked him, "What power of attorney is that?"

He shot me a surprised look as he replied, "I assumed you knew about it. He has given you full power of attorney."

"Who has?"

"Valentinius, of course."

"Why?"

"Why?" He was getting flustered. "So that you may act in his place during his absence."

"Where'd he go?"

"You *are* Ashton Ford." It was a question, expressed as a declaration. His eyes strayed briefly to the jottings in his legal notebook. I was picking up his mental wavelength. Confusion was there, also an occasional flare of impatience and maybe hostility. Even some fear perhaps. "Surely you know why you are here."

I smiled, told him, "I know nothing about why I am here, even less about your client."

"So why *are* you here?"

"I was invited."

"But you don't know why?"

"That's right. I don't know why. And I do not know any Valentinius de Medici."

Sloane's synapses were flaring like crazy now. And he was losing the lawyerly demeanor. "Well this is insane, purely insane. Why would the man empower you to act in his behalf if . . . if . . ."

I replied, "My thought exactly. Why doesn't he empower you? How long have you represented him?"

He said, "Our firm does have limited powers of attorney. For many years. But . . . have you never met Mr. de Medici?"

"Not sure," I said. "Have you?"

"This is purely insane," Sloane declared.

"Possibly," I agreed. "How many years?"

"What?"

"You said you'd been his attorney for many years. How many is that?"

"He's our senior client."

"Meaning?"

"It's a family firm. My grandfather established it. We have always had the Medici account. May have been our very first client, very possibly our only client in the beginning."

"But you've never met the client."

"That's right," the lawyer replied with obvious discomfort. "But that's not so unusual. I mean my father always directly handled the business, and his father before him. I've only just recently become involved in . . ."

I quietly inquired, "Did your father die?"

Sloane replied, "He has become incapacitated."

"Ill?"

"Ill, yes—institutionalized. I am now the senior partner."

"You said a family firm. Is it still . . . ?"

"Yes. We—wait a minute—what the hell is this? I get the feeling I'm under examination. Let's get this—"

I had been reading the power of attorney. I waved it at the young lawyer and told him, "*I* am now the client you know. I can fire your ass, with all the force and power of de Medici himself. So let's keep this discussion on the proper level."

Sloane glared at me for a moment, eyes dancing and mind whirling—then I began getting nicely harmonized thought patterns as he relaxed into his chair with a soft laugh. "You know, you're right."

"Who witnessed this document?"

"Our senior legal secretary. That's her notary stamp."

"So she knows de Medici?"

"Well . . . not exactly. But he presented proper identification. And his signature checked out."

"Who prepared the document?"

"She did. De Medici dictated it by telephone, came in later to execute it. Meanwhile I had gone over it, found it okay and—"

"When was this?"

"Just this afternoon. Well, more like noontime when he called it in. I approved the form and went to lunch. He came in and executed the document while I was out. He also left me a message to get this stuff out here as quickly as possible."

"Where is your office located?"

"We're in Santa Ana, near the court house."

"So it took you about . . .?"

"Well it can be an hour's drive, this time of day. I came right out."

"What else do you have there?"

"Various records and documents related to the problem."

I lit a cigarette, studied the smoke for a moment, asked, "What problem is that?"

He said, "This is very weird. Are you saying that you know *nothing* about . . .?"

I suggested, "Let's say that is the case. I'm totally ignorant. Let's educate me."

The lawyer sighed, stared disapprovingly at my cigarette smoke, ran a hand through his hair, sighed again. The synaptical firings were getting a bit out of sync when he pushed back his chair, crossed his legs, folded his hands in his lap, told me: "The state of California is making a move on this property."

"What kind of move? Eminent domain?"

"No. Well sort of, but . . . actually there is a legal question of proper succession to title. It's all very weird and baffling, and . . ."

I was going through the other documents, just scanning them to get some sensing of what was there. Original

Spanish land grant, or a copy thereof, dated 1782; validation by the new Mexican government in 1835; successive recordings and validations as California further mutated politically into the modern age.

I commented, "Looks like a lock to me. Goes back for over two hundred years."

"Well, yes, there's no question in the early abstract," Sloane replied. "The problem is, uh, you see . . ." He was thumbing through the historical abstract of title, trying to read it upside down, finally placing his finger at the crucial point. "Look at this date."

The entry was dated August 4, 1921. It recorded the final adjustment to the original land parcel, which once had encompassed thousands of acres but now was confined to the headland jutting into the Pacific, the present boundaries.

I said, "Yes?"

"Yes. Please note the date. Note also the name on the entitlement."

The name was recorded as Valentinius de Medici.

I said, "Okay."

He said, "Look at the name on the original grant."

I did. Again, the name was Valentinius de Medici.

I said, "Okay. Same family."

He said, "The Valentinius who recorded the 1921 deed is the final Valentinius of record."

I said, "Okay."

"He is the one who retained my grandfather's legal services in 1918."

"Okay."

"He was middle-aged at the time."

"Your grandfather?"

"Valentinius. My grandfather wasn't even thirty yet."

I was looking more closely into the documents. They reflected a long de Medici line.

Sloane sighed, his mental wavelength went almost flat, and he told me, "This guy has got to be over a hundred years old."

"Yeah?"

"Yeah. Or else the state of California has a hell of a good case."

I said, "What *is* their case?"

"They are taking the position that the owner of record has died intestate and without natural heirs."

I said, "Now wait a minute."

"Therefore the property passes legally to the state. We have got to produce Mr. de Medici, alive and fully documented as the owner of record, within ten days from today."

"Ten days, eh."

"Frankly, I have been wondering if it is possible to do that. I am beginning to wonder even, if my own father is not somehow involved in some conspiracy to . . . look here, Ford, I have a right to the facts in this case. Valentinius refuses to come forward. Instead he advances you as his proxy. So you must know what is going on here."

I said, "I haven't the foggiest, pal. How hard have you tried to find this guy?"

"I have spent the past year exhausting every avenue. I even traced the family line back to Renaissance Italy. I have found only one record of birth for a Valentinius de

Medici, and not a single record of death. Yet the name keeps—"

"Back to when?"

"What?"

"What is the date of that record of birth?"

"The year is 1690, in Italy."

I sighed, lit another cigarette, reminded my disturbed lawyer, "You said a hundred years old. Sounds more like three hundred years old to me. Is there a problem with that?"

He said, "It's no time for jokes. Of course I have a problem with that."

So did I. Because I was beginning to get a glimmer of why I had been "invited" to Pointe House. I told the lawyer, "Not joking. I meant, if I could produce this three-hundred-year-old man for the court's inspection, would that help your case?"

"I hope to hell you're joking," Sloane said.

But I was not.

Like the man said, it was no time for jokes. I understood the ten-day crisis now.

And I was just wondering exactly what I was supposed to pull off within ten days.

FIVE

A Possible Impossibility

There is a story that is told and persistently repeated in the literature of the period, concerning a mysterious and influential figure with intimate access to the royal courts of Europe during the eighteenth and nineteenth centuries, who charmed and astounded the nobility of the Continent for more than one hundred years, and perhaps directly influenced the actual history of the period.

The man was the almost legendary Comte de St. Germain, believed to be the son of Prince Franz-Leopold Ragoczy and heir to the throne of the principality of Siebenburgen (Transylvania). The principality was swallowed by the Austrain Empire in the late seventeenth century and St. Germain, as a boy of seven, was thought to have been spirited away and raised under the personal protection of the last Grand Duke of Tuscany, the Duc de Medici. This region of Italy, which includes Florence, Pisa, and Siena, became the greatest center of Renaissance culture under the Medici family, who ruled Tuscany for three hundred years, provided the church with three popes, and became linked by marriage to the royal families of Europe. The Medicis are regarded as perhaps the most prominent patrons of the arts in European history.

It is possible that St. Germain was a Medici, but his direct lineage—if this biography is accurate—was to the throne at Transylvania. It is possible also that the legend which arose around the man was the direct inspiration for the 1897 Gothic novel, *Dracula*, by Irish writer Bram Stoker, in which a Transylvanian count has achieved immortality via vampirism.

I have found no suggestion that St. Germain was ever regarded as a vampire or werewolf, but he was clearly held in awe by all who were exposed to him. Apparently he traveled all over Europe, to Africa, India, and China, and spent several years at the court of the shah of Persia. He was a familiar figure in the lives of Louis XV and Louis XVI, Madame de Pompadour and Marie Antoinette of France; of Peter III and Catherine II of Russia; apparently he knew such diverse personages as Tchaikovsky and Voltaire, merchants and princes and artists, scientists and philosophers.

It was written of him by a contemporary: "The Count speaks French, English, German, Italian, Spanish and Portuguese equally perfectly; so much so that when he converses with any of the inhabitants of the above countries in their mother tongue, they are unable to discover the slightest foreign accent. The Learned and the Oriental scholars have proved the knowledge of the Count St. Germain. The former found him more apt in the languages of Homer and Virgil than themselves; with the latter he spoke Sanskrit, Chinese, Arabic in such a manner as to show them that he had made some lengthy stay in Asia, and that the languages of the East were but poorly learned in the Colleges of Louis The Great and Montaigne."

According to the record, St. Germain was greatly talented in all the arts. He was a composer and an extraordinary musician, a painter who astonished with his remarkably brilliant colors, and a scholar with astounding knowledge.

"The Comte de St. Germain accompanied on the piano without music, not only every song but also the most difficult concerti, played on various instruments. Rameau was much impressed with the playing of this dilettante, and especially struck at his improvising.

"The Count paints beautifully in oils; but that which makes his paintings so remarkable is a particular colour, a secret, which he has discovered, and which lends to the painting an extraordinary brilliancy. Vanloo, who never tires in his admiration of the surprising colouring, has often requested the Count to let him participate in his secret; the latter, however, will not divulge it.

"Without attempting to sit in judgement on the knowledge of a fellow-being, of whom at this very moment that I am writing, both court and town have exhausted all surmises, one can, I think, well assert that a portion of his miracles is due to his knowledge of physics and chemistry in which sciences he is well grounded. At all events it is palpable that his knowledge has laid the seeds for him of sound good health; a life which will—or which has— overstepped the ordinary time allotted to man; and has also endowed him with the means of preventing the ravages of time from affecting the body."

That last sentence quoted is most interesting and most pertinent to our own story, as is the following account: "There appeared at the Court [of Louis XV] in these days an extraordinary man, who called himself Comte de St. Germain. At first he distinguished himself through his cleverness and the great diversity of his talents, but in another respect he soon aroused the greatest astonishment.

"The old Countess v. Georgy who fifty years earlier had accompanied her husband to Venice where he had the appointment of ambassador, lately met St. Germain at Mme. de Pompadour's. For some time she watched the stranger with signs of the greatest surprise, in which was mixed not a little fear. Finally, unable to control her excitement, she approached the Count more out of curiosity than in fear.

" 'Will you have the kindness to tell me,' said the Countess, 'whether your father was in Venice about the year 1710?'

" 'No, Madame,' replied the Count quite unconcerned, 'it is very much longer since I lost my father; but I myself was living in Venice at the end of the last and the beginning of this century; I had the honour to pay you court then, and you were kind enough to admire a few Barcarolles of my composing which we used to sing together.'

" 'Forgive me, but that is impossible; the Comte de St.

Germain I knew in those days was at least forty-five years old, and you, at the outside, are that age at present.'

"'Madame,' replied the Count smiling, 'I am very old.'

"'But then you must be nearly one hundred years old!'

"'That is not impossible.' And then the Count recounted to Mme. v. Georgy a number of familiar little details which had reference in common to both, to their sojourn in the Venitian States. He offered, if she still doubted him, to bring back to her memory certain circumstances and remarks, which—

"'No, no,' interrupted the old ambassadress, 'I am already convinced. For all that you are a most extraordinary man, a devil.'

"'For pity's sake!' exclaimed St. Germain in a thundering voice, 'no such names!'

"He appeared to be seized with a cramp-like trembling in every limb, and left the room immediately.

"I mean to get to know this peculiar man more intimately. St. Germain is of medium height and elegant manners; his features are regular; his complexion brown; his hair black; his face mobile and full of genius; his carriage bears the impress and the nobility common only to the great. The Count dresses simply but with taste. His only luxury consists of a large number of diamonds, with which he is fairly covered; he wears them on every finger, and they are set in his snuffboxes and his watches. One evening he appeared at court with shoebuckles, which Herr v. Gontaut, an expert on precious stones, estimated at 200,000 Francs."

Another contemporary view places St. Germain in England during the Jacobite revolution of 1745. In a letter to a friend in Florence, Horace Walpole, Earl of Oxford, writes: "The other day they seized an odd man who goes by the name of Count St. Germain. He has been here these two years, and will not tell who he is or whence, but professes that he does not go by his right name. He sings and plays on the violin wonderfully, is mad, and not very sensible."

Apparently the authorities had suspected St. Germain of revolutionary activities, but he was quickled released with full apologies and entertained at dinner by William Stanhope, Earl of Harrington, Secretary of the Treasury. Commenting on this incident, the *British Gazetteer* further elaborated: "The author of the Brussels' Gazette tells us that the person who styles himself Comte de St. Germain, who lately arrived here from Holland, was born in Italy in 1712. He speaks German and French as fluently as Italian, and expresses himself pretty well in English. He has a smattering of all the arts and sciences, is a good chemist, a virtuoso in musick, and a very agreeable companion."

It seems that the mystery man lived as a prince in Vienna for a year or two, close friend to Prince Ferdinand von Lobkowitz who was first minister to Emperor Francis I. He traveled Europe with the wealthy grandson of Fouquet, Marechal de Belle-Isle, who was "strongly taken with the brilliant and witty St. Germain," and went to India with British General Clive and Vice Admiral Watson. Louis XV assigned him a suite of rooms at his royal Chateau of Chambord and outfitted an experimental laboratory in which St. Germain taught certain skills to an august assemblage of students that included such as the Baron de

Gleichen, the Marquise d'Urfe, and the Princess of Anhalt-Zerbst (mother of Catherine II of Russia).

The *Gazette of the Netherlands* reported in 1761: "The so-called Count of St. Germain is an incomprehensible man of whom nothing is known: neither his name nor his origin, nor his position; he has an income, no one knows from whence it is derived; acquaintances, no one knows where he made them; entry into the Cabinets of Princes without being acknowledged by them!

"Letters from Paris state that when starting for this country, to which he came without asking permission of the King, M. de St. Germain returned his Red Ribbon: but it is practically certain that he has an understanding with the King of Denmark."

The British Museum was the repositor of pieces of music composed by the Comte de St. Germain in 1745 and 1760, and Prince Ferdinand von Lobkowitz's library in the castle of Raudnitz in Bohemia proudly displayed a personally autographed book of music by St. Germain, where it was said that he was a splendid violinist and "played like an orchestra."

He has been linked closely to the cause of the German-born empress of Russia, Catherine the Great, and perhaps to the political intrigue that enthroned her in 1762. Catherine's thirty-four-year reign was the most enlightened in Russian history, and it was her vision that led an emerging Russia into closer participation in the politics and culture of Europe. St. Germain is credited in a contemporary writing as having "played a great part in their revolution," and is mentioned in an anonymous 1869 publication titled: "A few Words about the First Helpers of Catherine II."

In 1763 a nobleman in Brussels, Graf (Count) Karl Cobenzl, in a letter to Prince Kaunitz, described St. Germain thusly: "It was about three months ago that the person known by the name of the Comte de St. Germain passed this way, and came to see me. I found him the most singular man that I ever saw in my life. I do not yet precisely know his birth; I believe, however, that he is the son of a clandestine union in a powerful and illustrious family. Possessing great wealth, he lives in the greatest simplicity; he knows everything, and shows an uprightness, a goodness of soul, worthy of admiration. Among a number of his accomplishments, he made, under my own eyes, some experiments, of which the most important were the transmutation of iron into a metal as beautiful as gold, and at least as good for all goldsmith's work; the dyeing and preparation of skins, carried to a perfection which surpassed all the moroccos in the world, and the most perfect tanning; the dyeing of silks, carried to a perfection hitherto unknown; the like dyeing of woollens; the dyeing of wood in the most brilliant colours penetrating through and through, and the whole without either indigo or cochineal, with the commonest ingredients, and consequently at a very moderate price; the composition of colours for painting, ultra-marine is as perfect as if made from lapis lazuli; and finally, removing the smell from painting oils, and making the best oil of Provence from the oils of Navette, of Colsat, and from others, even the worst. I have in my hands all these productions, made under my own eyes; I have had them undergo the most strict examinations, and seeing in these articles a profit which mount up to millions, I have endeavoured to take advantage of the friendship that this man has felt for me, and to learn from him all these secrets."

Dieudonne Thiebault writes in about the year 1769: "There came to Berlin and remained in that city for the space of a year a remarkable man, who passed by the name of the Comte de St. Germain. The Abbe Pernety was not slow in recognising in him the characteristics which go to make up an adept, and came to us with wonderful stories." Princess Amelie called on St. Germain in Berlin, and Thiebault remarks that the aged Baron Knyhausen was always addressed by St. Germain as "my son."

Thiebault describes the mysterious traveler: "In appearance M. de St. Germain was refined and intellectual. He was clearly of gentle birth, and had moved in good society; and it was reported that the famous Cagliostro (so well known for his mystification of Cardinal Rohan and others at Paris) had been his pupil. The pupil, however, never reached the level of his master and, while the latter finished his career without mishap, Cagliostro was often rash to the point of criminality, and died in the prison of the Inquisition at Rome. In the history of M. de St. Germain, we have the history of a wise and prudent man who never wilfully offended against the code of honour, or did aught that might offend our sense of probity. Marvels we have without end, never anything mean or scandalous."

A Florence news item published in *Le notizie del Mondo* carries a report from Tunis, July 1770: "The Comte Maximilian de Lamberg, Chamberlain of M.M.L.L. II. and RR having paid a visit to the Island of Corsica to make various investigations, has been staying here since the end of June, in company with the Signor de St. Germain, celebrated in

Europe for the vastness of his political and philosophical knowledge."

Writing from the Netherlands some years later, Heer van Sypesteyn said, "M. de St. Germain came to the Hague after the death of Louis XV [May 10th, 1774] and left for Schwalbach in 1774. This was the last time he visited Holland. It cannot be ascertained with accuracy how often he was there. It is stated in a German biography that he was in Holland in 1710, 1735, 1742, 1748, 1760 and 1773."

And how did the Dutch regard St. Germain? ". . . a remarkable man, and wherever he was personally known he left a favourable impression behind, and the remembrance of many good and sometimes of many noble deeds. Many a poor father of a family, many a charitable institution, was helped by him in secret. Not one bad, nor one dishonourable action was ever known of him, and so he inspired sympathy everywhere, and not least in Holland."

I trust that this is quite enough about St. Germain. But I have to give you just a bit more. Like this little gem: "Sometimes he fell into a trance, and when he again recovered, he said he had passed the time while he lay unconscious in far-off lands; sometimes he disappeared for a considerable time, then suddenly re-appeared, and let it be understood that he had been in another world in communication with the dead."

Okay?

Please note the "disappeared" and "suddenly re-appeared" in the quote just above.

Had you ever heard of the Comte de St. Germain before this? Probably not. Isn't it just a little strange that such a remarkable character could escape the notice of our historians? Probably not. We do not give a lot of space in our histories to the truly remarkable characters; none at all to the likes of a St. Germain.

One final note, this from the *Souvenirs de Marie Antoinette* by an intimate friend of the queen, the Countess d'Adhemar. The *Souvenirs* are based on the countess's daily diary. She was an intimate within the royal court, and she had a sense of history. She also had a remarkable friend who had labored heroically to save the royal family from their grisly fate. The following entry refers to a perilous visit by St. Germain in 1792 after the French monarchy had toppled:

"The church was empty; I posted my Laroche as sentinel and I entered the chapel named; soon after, and almost before I had collected my thoughts in the presence of God, behold a man approaching . . . it was himself in person . . . Yes! with the same countenance as in 1760, while mine was covered with furrows and marks of decrepitude . . . I stood impressed by it; he smiled at me, came forward, took my hand, kissed it gallantly. I was so troubled that I allowed him to do it in spite of the sanctity of the place.

"'There you are!' I said. 'Where have you come from?'

"'I am come from China and Japan. . . .'

"'Or rather from the other world!'

"'Yes, indeed, pretty nearly so! Ah! Madame, down there nothing is so strange as what happens here. How is the monarchy of Louis XIV disposed of? You, who did not see it cannot make the comparison, but I . . .'

"'I have caught you, man of yesterday!'"

Man of yesterday, indeed. Louis XIV's reign had ended nearly one hundred years earlier.

Early on, St. Germain had tried to warn Louis XVI and Marie Antoinette of the coming upheaval. The crown would not listen, and now—with all of the nobility in great jeopardy—St. Germain had come to counsel his friend, Madame d'Adhemar. As he bid farewell to the Countess, she asked him whether she would see him again. He replied, "Five times more; do not wish for the sixth." He then stepped through the doorway and disappeared into thin air; literally, according to her account.

Louis XVI and Marie Antoinette were both beheaded in the year 1793, Louis in January and his queen in August.

Now, this fragment from *Souvenirs*: "I saw M. de St. Germain again, and always to my unspeakable surprise: at the assassination of the Queen; at the coming of the 18th Brumaire; the day following the death of the Duke d'Enghien [1804]; in the month of January, 1813; and on the eve of the murder of the Duke de Berri [1820]. I await the sixth visit when God wills." Countess d'Adhemar died of natural causes in 1822.

So okay. We have but a tiny glimpse here of a living phenomenon—first noted in about 1710 as a man in his forties, finally in the year 1820 as a man who shows no evidence of aging.

So are we ready now for Valentinius?

Or are we talking about the same guy?

SIX

Second Sight

Of course I was just flailing about for a handle, any handle, and St. Germain came to mind only because of his supposed linkage to the Medici family of Renaissance Italy. Actually I knew very little of the St. Germain legend at the time, and I had to allow for the possible coincidence of names, even though Sloane had traced our California Medici (or his forebears) to the eighteenth-century Florentine duchy. The original Valentinius would have been a contemporary of St. Germain and apparently came to these shores shortly after the American Revolution with a Spanish land grant in his pocket. It could be significant, or merely coincidental, that the Medici family had marriage links to the Spanish throne.

But after all, how much coincidence can you buy? I was into some pretty heady stuff. The name *Valentinius* itself evokes all sorts of images, being a slight variation on three Roman emperors—Valentinian I, II, and III, a pope, Valentinus, ninth century, and an earlier Valentinus of the second century A.D. who was a Christian mystic and founder of the Roman and Alexandrian schools of Gnosticism. For a further small variation, the Latin title for those three Roman emperors is *Flavius Valentinianus*—so it appears that small variations were not considered a problem in those days. We should be aware that family names have not always been as formalized as they are today; in fact, they did not even come into vogue until the late Middle Ages.

Remember too that I was being confronted with one hell of an anomaly. The guy who winked-in on me at Malibu was apparently the same guy who'd given me an unlimited power of attorney to save, I guessed, the remnants of a two-hundred-year-old Spanish land grant from being confiscated by the modern state of California.

So put yourself in my moccasins please, and tell me why I should not be reaching at wild conclusions.

Still it would not be accurate to say that I was *reaching* for anything at all; I was merely reacting to quivers and going with the flow.

Jim Sloane however obviously wanted me to start a flow of my own. "It seems that the ball is in your court," he observed. "What do you intend to do with it?"

I replied, "No, Jim; the ball is not yet in my court." We were talking tennis terms, and I was in my element there. "Someone has just handed me a racquet and pushed me toward the court. And I think this racquet needs to be restrung. I'd rather use my own."

He smiled faintly and said, "Fine, use whatever you'd

like but do it quick. The finals are a week from Friday, and it's winner-take-all."

He closed his briefcase and rose to leave; offered me his hand and I took it. I told him, "The handshake is pure courtesy. I'm agreeing only to look into the thing. I'll contact you within twenty-four hours to let you know whether I'm accepting the game. The state of California is a hell of an opponent. And I don't even know who is sponsoring this match."

Sloane said, "My guess says Hank Gibson is sponsoring it."

I asked, "Who is Hank Gibson and what is his interest?"

The lawyer stared at me for a moment, as though reflecting on that, then told me: "Gibson is the latest and greatest boy entrepreneur financial genius of Orange County. Real estate speculator. As you must know, oceanfront property is hard to come by in this area and therefore it comes at a heavy premium. Gibson was in contact with my father last year shortly before the state filed its action —hounded the hell out of him in fact, trying to get in touch with Medici. I don't know what kind of a deal he was brokering, but you can bet your ass it would have been highly profitable for the boy wonder. Anyway, his efforts failed. The state began its move a few weeks after Gibson bowed out. But I have had to wonder if he actually did give it up. There are all sorts of stories about Gibson's influence at Sacramento."

Sure, that was interesting. I asked Sloane, "Are you suggesting that this guy expects to buy the property from the state if it is confiscated?"

He replied, "No, I'm suggesting that the deal may already be set. Gibson is not a developer; he's a broker. However the property may ultimately find its way into a developer's hands, it could mean a fat fee for the boy wonder."

I said, "I detect some personal animosity between you two. Am I right?"

The lawyer flash-smiled, picked up his briefcase, and went to the door; turned back to say in parting, "You bet there is."

It was about five o'clock that afternoon when I invaded Francesca's studio in a search of some light on the goings-on at Pointe House. But she wasn't there, so I browsed her art instead and found it quite good. I am no judge of fine art but I know what I like, and I liked most of her stuff, though I would have a tough time describing her style to a critic. Representational rather than abstract certainly, but even her seascapes revealed abstract symbols at close look; romantic, rather than baroque, but there were definite baroque touches, even in a couple of portraits; more coloristic in style than linear, but also highly perspective with deep shifts and flowing currents of color in, say, a background sky or sea.

The colors were what really got to me, I guess, so I would have to say that color was the most distinctive characteristic of her work. And yet, something else leaped out from some of the stuff—some quality of feeling or emotion—I mean some special *grabbing* but totally ethereal representation; such as in a compelling study of a mother whale and her baby, the juxtaposition of mother and offspring in a way that spoke to me of mother-love and child-like-faith, of nurturing and being nurtured.

The lady was good. Damned good.

As for her sculptures, what could I say except to note the startling realism, the total imprint of character upon a lump of clay, the projection of personality frozen like a single frame of movie film, yet containing all the inner attributes of the subject. Like, you could look at this sculpted head and know what makes the subject laugh and what makes him cry. I knew Valentinius better from one of those clay busts than from the eyeball confrontation in Malibu.

And I think I was getting to know a little something about the artist, too, much more than our personal meeting had provided. Art is like that, sometimes, whatever the medium, the artist revealing more of self than anything else in the work.

I spent about ten minutes becoming abstractly acquainted with Francesca Amalie, then I wandered to a telescope at the window and peered at a couple of sailboats, inspected the mountains of Catalina Island thirty or so miles offshore, watched a seal slither off a rock into the sea just below—at which time Francesca herself strolled into the focal field. Took my breath away. She was nude, on the beach, yet close as my eyeball and as immediate as the air I inhaled. I shamelessly watched her cross to a blanket on the sands and lie down, then I abandoned the telescope and went searching for Hai Tsu.

I found my hostess in a tidy apartment behind the kitchen. It was small but as luxurious from the doorway as anything else I'd seen at the mansion. She did not invite me in but greeted me with her usual restrained joy, then asked, "How may we serve you?"

I replied, "Any way you wish, ma'am," but she did not react to that, so I limped on with: "Uh, I thought I saw Francesca on the beach. How do I get down there?"

She smiled graciously, said, "I will show," and I followed her through the house to the atrium, a garden under glass which serves as the main entry hall to the mansion. I thought we were headed outside but she opened a narrow door on the north wall, smiled, and needlessly pointed out: "Elevator."

I thanked her and she left me there.

It was an open-cage type, quite old but automated and sturdy enough, as smooth as any modern elevator I'd ever used. There were only two buttons, UP and DOWN, so there was no need for a directory. I descended through a shaft of sheer rock walls, like coming down off the top of a fifteen- or twenty-story building, and emerged into muted sunshine on a south-facing ledge some twenty-five feet above the ocean. Steps scooped from the rock took me the rest of the way to the beach of a small cove facing Laguna. Mean high tide be damned, this beach was totally private by virtue of its inaccessibility except by boat or elevator. No more than fifty feet wide by twenty feet deep, it was carved out of coastal rock and isolated by soaring escarpments rising from deep water to either side. A couple of seals were snoozing in the sun and a pelican ruffled his wings and checked me out from his perch on a small rock at the center of the beach; otherwise it was just she and me and the deep blue sea, the roar of the surf breaking on the rocks that formed this cove.

She looked at me and I looked at she for quite a long moment before she decorously covered herself with a short robe and made me welcome. I dropped to the blanket beside her and lay back to gaze at the sky as I quietly inquired, "How'd you know I'd come?"

She laughed lightly, not exactly a giggle but with a touch of nervousness, then asked, "How do you know I wanted you to come?"

I said, "You sent the elevator back topside for me."

She said, "Boy, what is that? Egotism or self-assurance? How do you know someone else wasn't down here before you, and *he* left the elevator topside?"

I said, "Valentinius would not need the elevator."

She said, "I guess not."

My arrival had disturbed the seals. I heard them slithering away. Then Francesca slithered aboard me. She'd left the robe behind, and my startled hands instantly became aware of that.

Love at first sight?

Well . . . lust, anyway. For damned sure lust.

SEVEN

Déjà What?

You can find love without sex and sex without love. The two together are nice, very nice; but even if you find either, without the oher, life is usually enhanced because you did. With neither life would be a terribly gray affair, and I am not sure I would want it.

But what the hell is love, exactly, and what is sex?

Try to consider the question from the God viewpoint. You're considering building a world out of matter and infusing the matter, here and there, with some subtle essence of yourself. Not from vanity: you are God, after all; what is there to be vain about when you are everything? No; you want to build because of an innate need for self-expression and there is no way to express yourself except to *create*. But what the hell to create? You're an artist without oils or canvas, a poet without words, a novelist with no heroic tales to tell, a composer without music.

Eureka! That's it! You will project all these creative aspects of yourself into an energy universe of space and time in which all the creative tools and circumstances may be developed for a full expression of your *self*!

But wait, wait . . . this is likely to become troublesome. I mean, we are talking a hell of a big production here. When we start talking space and time, energy and matter, creative tools and artful expression . . . well it's going to take quite a bang to get something like that started. And once it's started, what's to control it? *Moi*? Let's think about this.

You just want a creative expression; you don't want to be tied down to governing and policing, housework and all that crap! So who's going to be the executive in charge of production of this big bang?

Aha! Okay. You are God so you have the answer within yourself. It's so obvious. You will deputize and delegate authority—sort of like hands-off management.

But wait. There is no deputy material here, nothing to delegate authority to.

But why not? If you can create a big bang, then surely you can create deputies and delegates. All you have to do. . . .

Well see, try it this way: just start the damned thing going; something will pop out of all that chaos, some aspect of your creative self that was projected into the bang will just naturally begin to stir sooner or later, and start to take charge. I mean, it will *assume* authority because you will project an authority aspect into the bang; just *thinking* it will make it so; so *think* creative authority.

Simple, isn't it.

Well it *seems* simple, but . . .

No sweat. Trust me. I'm your higher-self aspect, and I know.

But . . . with all that *creative authority* running around loose out there. . . . Aren't we asking for sheer chaos, all manner of conflict, maybe even anarchy and revolution?

That's the risk you take. But . . .

Yes?

Well . . . as a control . . . why don't you try projecting a bit of love aspect into the bang.

Surely you jest! Come on now. Love? You want me to give my *love* to this project?

Why not? You have plenty to go around.

But . . . you are giving me palpitations. I mean you don't know what you're saying! *Love* is *Godly*! If I put *love* in there . . . oh I think I see what you're getting at. Yes. But uh . . . that's a lot of power. How can we be sure that one of those deputies won't just keep it all to himself? I mean, you know, hoard the aspect and refuse to share it with the other delegates.

Give them sex.

Oh come on now! We can't give them *sex*! Creative I could allow, okay but not *pro*creative!

Why not? That makes mortality part of the package, so it minimizes the power plays and keeps love flowing along. I'm your higher-self aspect; trust me.

So God gave love and sex to his creation.

So why is it so damned hard to find a little sometimes? You tell me why.

I am sure that everyone who may read this report has encountered the term *déjà vu*, and most have probably had the experience; many however do not fully understand what may be happening there, so let me take a moment to discuss it. Translated literally from the French, it means "already seen." But what the term was designed to describe is a phenomenon involving seeing, hearing, or even thinking something—often accompanied by a shivery feeling—that has already happened and appears to be happening again in the precisely same way.

Say that you are on the streets of a strange city and you approach an intersection where you know you have never walked before; you round a corner, and in the split second *before* you can see around the corner, you already know what lies beyond. Everything you then see comes at you with a rush of familiarity—perhaps even the odors and sounds peculiar to that particular street scene.

Or you may be seated in your own home in casual conversation with old friends (or new acquaintances); one person makes a statement, and as another replies you suddenly *know* that you had heard the reply before it was uttered; that moreover, you have been through this entire experience before and it all seems to be happening again.

That is déjà vu. It is really a very common human experience in its simpler forms, but there are also deeply complex forms of déjà vu, which we shall see later.

These simple déjà vus are explained in various ways

depending upon who is pontificating at the moment. A view popular in psychology would explain the phenomenon as a trick played on us by the brain. In this argument it is theorized that sensory stimuli scattering through the gray matter at light-speed and organized into a perceptive bundle at some point is sometimes organized *twice* and therefore perceived twice, the second time almost like an echo following very closely on the heels of the first. We therefore get a "double print," the second perception arriving before we have had time to assimilate the first and blending into it in a most deceptive way.

To my knowledge no one has yet demonstrated the echo effect in a laboratory, so the theory is no more valid than any other.

A parapsychologist would probably tell you that your déjà vu was a precognitive flash, while the metaphysician would prefer that you think of it as having something to do with past-life recall or a momentary hole in the mystical curtain that separates you from omniscience. None of that has been demonstrated under wires either, so you can come to your own conclusions without fear of being soundly contradicted.

The reason some people connect déjà vu to past-life recall is that there are certain similarities in the more complex forms. Take the case of an eight-year-old girl who arrives in a certain neighborhood or a certain village or town for the first time; upon seeing it, she becomes highly excited and begins pointing out familiar scenes; perhaps she leaps from the car at a certain point and begins running from house to house searching for someone she could never have seen before in this lifetime—*and finds them*!

Whoa...

That's pretty heavy, sure, but numerous similar experiences have been reported in the record of our times.

I have my own theory about déjà vu, but I'm keeping it to myself for now.

I bring it all up at this point merely to try to provide some perspective on my experience with Francesca Amalie on the beach below Pointe House. I didn't know what happened there. I did know that the whole mind-blowing happening unfolded as a sustained spine-tingling sense of déjà vu such as I had never before experienced; I mean from the moment I stepped off the elevator until the moment we lay gasping for breath twenty feet off the blanket and shivering in the cold spreading fingers of the Pacific; I was reliving, not living, the experience on a frame-by-frame basis, and not just with the mind but with the whole crazy body vibrating to the double-print sensations and girding itself hungrily for the spectacular double-print climax that had to be approaching in two worlds at once. Oh God, what beauty! What peace with frenzy and what frenzy with peace! What utter *adoration* of another living being!—both ways, that adoration was flowing both ways between the bodies.

Call it an act of love or merely an act of sex; call it what you please; to me it was a mystical experience broadcasting through the flesh, and I had intimations of things during that frantic mating that cannot be expressed in mere human terms. I knew momentarily the pure bliss that is Godly love in its finest essence, and I learned meaning of rapture. I believe I also learned something about sexual love.

But I didn't know what the hell was really going on there. At the moment I did not particularly give a damn.

When we found the strength to do so, we returned to the blanket and bundled on it, shivering not just from the cold but also in the memory of that sexual union.

After a while, quite a long while of snuggling and quiet rumination, Francesca whispered to me, "I'm sorry that I lied to you."

I asked, "When did you do that?"

She replied without pause, "I did not come to Pointe House one year ago."

So I had to ask her, "When did you come, then?"

"I came," she told me, in a flat, matter-of-fact reply, "the first time, in 1872."

Okay. I thought about that for a second or two, then observed, "It was built in 1921."

She said, "This is the third Pointe House. The first was built in 1798."

Uh huh.

"Who built it?"

"Valentinius built it. It was destroyed by fire in 1820. He again raised it in 1871 and brought me here a year later."

"Brought you here from where?"

"I had been staying in Vienna."

I said, "That makes you at least a hundred years older than me."

She said, "That is not impossible."

I said, "I see."

But I did not see, and I did not wish to see. So I tried to lighten it up a bit.

I asked, "Are you then the bride of Dracula?"

She laughed. Just laughed.

But I, pal, was anything but laughing.

EIGHT

Reverse View

I should have pursued the question while the mood was there, but I was not emotionally prepared to do that at the moment, and the whole thing had slipped away by the time we returned to the house. I mean, the whole thing. We were back to where we'd been at our first meeting. It was as though there were two Francescas, one for frolicking on the beach and the other distant and absorbed in the preoccupations of a totally different life.

"Can I take you to dinner?" I asked her as we left the elevator.

"I'll probably just have a bite in my studio," she replied noncommittally, but it was a clear signal.

I told her, "I like your work. Checked it out before I went below. Good stuff. How long have you been at it?"

"Obviously not long enough," she said, turning back the

compliment and evading the question with the one response.

Different girl, yeah.

So I left it there, for the moment, and went on to my suite. I heard water running in my bathroom and went through to check it out. Hai Tsu was in there, drawing a bath in the sunken tub. I backed away before she could see me and went to the bedroom window to collect my thoughts.

But it was a difficult collection.

Look, I'm no amateur at intrigue. I was raised in it, got a couple of damned degrees in it, and I'd practiced it as a professional in some of the toughest theaters on earth. But I did not know what to make of this present situation.

Sure, you're probably thinking at this point, what's the big deal? Some guy pulled a stage magician's trick on you at Malibu, got your attention in a way designed to lure you to Laguna and involve you in a conspiracy to defraud the state of California, further bedazzled you with some worthless papers and a ridiculous story of a man who would not die, then cinched the con with a dazzling seductress who fucked more than your body. She's playing the game, Ash; she's part of the con, and she has scrambled your brains.

So okay, I take all that under advisement.

But why me? And who could concoct such a bizarre con?—and how could anyone smart enough to concoct such a scenario not be smart enough to concoct one with a better success factor built into it?

Sure, I go to the movies, just like you; I've probably seen all the ones you've seen. I know, I know. So if it's not a con, then it's a nut house. I've joined the inmates. But is insanity contagious? Did I catch it from Francesca down there at Pointe Beach a while ago? Or was I already lost even before I went down there?

Had I been crazy all my life?

Was that the answer to Ashton Ford or Ford Ashton or whoever the hell I am?

I opened the little overnight kit I'd brought to Laguna from Malibu and took another look at that ten grand. It was real money. I'd brought it with me, in the thought that I could give it back if I did not like the case.

I did not like the case.

Frankly, I was scared of the damned case.

I wrapped the money in the power of attorney and returned it to the kit. I would give it to Jim Sloane. Not tomorrow. Tonight. I would take that bath which Hai Tsu was presumably drawing for me, shake the sand out of my clothes, and get the hell away from Pointe House while the getting was good.

I would take the bath, yeah, but it was not to be alone.

Hai Tsu had come up behind me. I knew she was there even before I turned around to confirm with the eyes what I already knew by some other avenue. Another dazzling seductress, yeah. I guess I knew at that very moment that the getting had already gone.

She wore a black, sheer, hip-length negligee, and that was all she wore other than a delicate red carnation in her hair. I had never cast eyes upon such a divine female form. This was almost a comic-strip body, calling up images of *Terry and the Pirates* and the Dragon Lady, except that this lady was definitely no dragon; this lady was God's own idea of feminine perfection.

She said to me, with that deliciously secretive joy in the quiet voice, "Bath is ready, Shen."

I was gawking, I know I was, but I was trying to at least gawk coolly. "What's that you called me?"

"Bath is ready," she repeated, reaching for me with a graceful gesture available only to women of the Orient.

Her hands were at my belt buckle and I was reaching for cool.

I said, "No, I mean, what name did you call me by?"

She was kneeling, withdrawing my pants, gazing up at me from across cosmos. "Call you Shen. Are you not Shen?"

I got it then. It had tickled a tendril of memory when Francesca told me earlier that Hai Tsu referred to Valentinius only as Shen, and explained, "I believe that is some kind of Oriental title of respect."

Now that tendril was flaring, and I knew that *Shen* was quite a bit more than a title of respect.

It has to do with the yin and the yang of Taoism, the interaction of which produces the created world and all that occurs within it. Yin is the passive, feminine principle and yang is the positive, masculine energy. Good spirits, collectively referred to as Shen, are full of yang.

Lao-tzu founded Taoism in the sixth century B.C. As a religion it lost much of its vitality after about the second century A.D. when it was combined with various elements of Buddhism, but survived strongly into twentieth-century China as a philosophy and also as a form of ceremonial magic.

In its magical forms the Tao is thought to be a route to immortality in the flesh. Early Taoist magicians were alchemists who compounded various substances in a search for immortality through chemistry (sort of like our modern medical researchers?), developed various potions and pills and combined it all with meditative disciplines designed to prolong life.

Lao-tzu is reputed to have possessed the secret of long life, and the Tao tradition speaks of the Three Isles of Immortality and the Eight Immortals who achieved immortality by ingesting certain substances.

See where I'm at now?

I'm a sunk duck, that's where I'm at, Shen or not.

Hai Tsu gently undressed me to the skin, then escorted me to the bath. But she did not put me in the tub right away. She first lay me down on the massage table, removed her negligee, uncoiled a hose from the bath fixture, and wet me down for a couple of minutes under a warm, gentle spray, both sides, then she used a large sponge and delicately perfumed soap to cover me front and back with a thick layer of foamy suds before she went to work on me with those incredible hands.

Yeah, I know where heaven's at.

I got a full body massage under delightfully slippery suds by trained hands that knew all the sensual paths to a man's heart; then I got a full body massage under the same delightfully slippery suds by another full body that knew how to fit all the opposing surfaces together in the most captivating maneuvers.

Ten minutes of that, pal, and you just don't give a shit anymore—not even with the enchanting Francesca less than an hour behind you. The yin is firmly in control of the yang, and all you have to do is lie back and let it happen.

It just went on happening for a greatly extended period of utter bliss—nothing explosive going on, you understand, just that same slow, sinuous, sensuous rubbing of flesh upon flesh. I couldn't even tell you if I had an erection during any of that; I wouldn't know and wouldn't care, wouldn't have given it a thought one way or another and it wouldn't have mattered one way or another.

Later, yeah, it mattered.

She knelt astride me on the table and thoroughly rinsed the suds from both of us with the warm spray; then she went to work on me with lips, teeth, and tongue—all of me, the whole extant surface area of me, nibbling and licking and kissing in that same slow, deliberate rhythm—and a whole lot of things quickly began to matter a whole lot.

This was the flip side of the Francesca experience. I mean that it was a reverse view—an opposite angle, so to speak—like the difference between inside and outside or topside and bottomside. It was a reverse view also in intensity. Where the one had been frantic, demanding, consuming, this one was languorous, lazy, a giving up and giving in, capitulation to the sense and immersion in pleasure.

Hai Tsu did not allow me an orgasm. She would lick, nibble, blow and tickle right up to the boundary of no-return then clamp and hold and divert sensations elsewhere, over and over—I don't know how many over and overs—just endlessly it seemed, until it gradually dawned on me that I was no longer straining to leap that boundary, or for anything whatever, and I slowly descended into the most relaxing peace I have ever known.

She wet me down again, turned on the whirlpool in the

tub, and softly announced, "Bath is ready, Shen. Dinner in one hour."

Then she quietly withdrew.

And so did I. I fell asleep, and dreamed miraculous dreams, and visited the Magi in a beautiful reverse view of the meaning of life and of death.

And knew in those dreams that both are the same.

NINE

The Echo and The Omen

The angel looked exactly like Valentinius but said his name was Valory, which I understood to be another cover identity for St. Germain. He told me that names are abstractions anyway, and serve their chief purpose as a legal convenience—hinting darkly that the human world is overly preoccupied with legalities—and suggested that I just call him Val for short.

I replied that I thought names were rather important abstractions at any rate, and that set him off on a long dissertation about the origin and customs of names and naming, implying that the thing had gone overboard and lost much of its meaning in the modern age.

He said look, in the beginning, before anyone had a

name, people had no trouble recognizing or dealing with one another. One look at a guy and you knew where he stood in the pecking order, whether he was boring or interesting, threatening or reassuring, and whether you'd care to dine with him. But then in order to communicate that attribute to a third person, you had to be able to refer to the guy, and you did so by his attribute.

Thus a chief may be referred to as Great One and a lackey as Kisses Ass, a rebel member as Hates Authority and a Lothario as Screws All.

See these are purely utilitarian abstracts of a personality —direct and to the point and *descriptive* in a way that leaves no doubt as to whom is being referred to since everyone in the tribe knows everyone else intimately even before the names are given. It is the *knowing* that determines what is given.

So names began as descriptions of personalities. All of the traditional names in use today owe their origin to that same idea but lost their directness when people started giving names to *babies*, before any definite attributes of character could be identified. The name given then became a hopeful attribute or a flattery to some other member of the tribe. So today we have *Michael*, which is from the Hebrew for *Who is Like God*, and *Avery*, Germanic for *Courageous*, or how about *Boyd*, Celtic for *Yellow-haired*.

I told Valory that I really did not give a damn about any of that, I just wondered why *he* had to have so damned many names and why couldn't he settle on just one?

He talked about names as titles and titles as names, like calling a judge "Your Honor" or a king "His Majesty"— how in this country we address our political leader as "Mr.

President"—and how those titles remain the same even though different personalities assume them—how church leaders assume new identities as they ascend to the papacy. He then returned to the earlier example and had Kisses Ass topple Great One and take over the tribe. Should their names remain the same? Or should they exchange names also, as they exchange roles?

I told him I guessed it did not really matter, so long as everyone knew who we were talking about. Then he brought up the question of posterity. Would the great-grandchildren of Screws All be able to follow the play of history if people were forever exchanging names as roles reversed? Probably not. So instead of exchanging names, it became the vogue to *change* names. Thus in the above scenario Kisses Ass topples Great One and becomes Great One II. He who was Great One becomes Vanquished.

I said okay.

He said, well, names still reflect history, you know, except now they have lost their directness and have no bearing on roles in current life. Family names especially simply reflect a line. A stock broker named Baker should be known as John the Broker, not John the Baker; a cook named Carpenter should be Carl the Cook, not Carl the Carpenter.

I told the angel it was just too confusing and it was giving me a headache. Let's just forget the whole thing.

He said, well, if I wished, but I really should not be called Ashton the Ford. He told me I have noble aspirations, and that in an earlier time those attributes could have led to a dukedom and I could have become known as Le Duc d'Malibu.

Ever notice how current experience can intrude on a dream? I had been thinking earlier, just before the bout with Hai Tsu, that I was a "sunk duck." I told Valory, in the dream, "That could be fun. Then my friends could refer to me as the *Sunk Duke*."

He chuckled and made some remark about everything being relative to everything else.

I said, sure, but titles like that just confused the matter further, and he agreed with me. "Precisely the point I hoped to make," he said.

It made no point whatever with me at the time, but I just let it pass.

Valory said, "So you can see the problem we have on *this* side."

I said, "Not really."

So he said, "Then come and let me show you."

We stepped into the elevator at Pointe House and Valory punched the DOWN button. The cage stayed where it was but *we* began descending along the shaft. We emerged not on the beach but into a huge hollow beneath Pointe House. You couldn't call this thing a cave; it took up the whole interior of the promontory and maybe even extended beyond—I couldn't see the end of it, just tier after tier and row upon row of greatly sophisticated hi-tech equipment. Looked like a mammoth Mission Control center with consoles and monitors, each monitor displaying a different scene or view, and each console manned by a uniformed figure who seemed very intent on the activities in his monitor.

I asked, "Are we launching Pointe House?"

Valory just smiled and we kept moving along a row of

consoles until I began to get the drift of this thing. It was like they were playing video tapes at those consoles, except I couldn't see any tape, just the array of controls at each console and the "movie" on the monitor.

But these were not movies.

Armies were clashing on those screens, men dying and women weeping in some strange overlay of scene upon scene in multiple superimpositions—like seeing an action while at the same time seeing all the fine ramifications of the action in the one view at the one time—occasional zoom-in close-ups of a frightened child or a dying man— but it was not all grim like that. There were other "movies" of happier scenes, triumphant scenes, birthings and birth-day parties and graduations, wedding scenes, all that. There were even very boring studies of men and women at work and at play, of lovers and dentists and athletes and all the things that go to make a human world.

I was beginning to understand.

I said to Valory, "This is the story of mankind."

Valory said to me, "Of all the mankinds. Past, present, and future of all the worlds. But not the story . . . the *record*."

I asked, "How do you record the future?"

He enigmatically explained, "The same as we record the present."

I said, "But if it hasn't happened yet . . ."

He said, "Who says it hasn't happened yet?"

I said, "Well if it's the *future* . . ."

He laughed and told me, "It is future there. But all is *now* here."

I thought about that for a moment, then said, "The *past* is now?"

"Sure."

"Then what is immortality?"

"Immortality is now."

"I thought it was forever."

"That too, Ashton. But forever is also now."

I was getting my headache again. I asked Valory, "What the hell does this have to do with names and naming?"

He replied, "To show you that there is no *now*."

I said, "Aw come on! You just said . . ."

He said, "All is process. The names record the process. See why we have such trouble with names? You are Ashton this time but you were Wolfgang another time and Eric still another; what is in the *name* Ashton, but an echo and an omen?"

Then he brought me before the Eight Immortals, and they were the Magi—and before I awoke, they showed me miracles and taught me that death is but another name for life. Each is an echo; each is an omen.

TEN

Nomenclature

You may be asking what is the big deal over names and naming. I was asking myself the same question as I put on fresh clothing from the magic closet and went down to dinner. But I quickly forgot all that the moment I got downstairs, because downstairs presented me with another array of questions.

Cocktails were being served in a lounge area just off the dining room. It was a large room and beautifully decorated with objets d'art and masterpieces to dignify any museum of fine art. Someone was playing beautifully on a concert grand in a corner of the room and several people were standing around it. Two nearly identical copies of Hai Tsu were moving about in quiet joy, attending to the needs of the moment. One of them greeted me with a Scotch on the rocks. I accepted it with the comment "How'd you know?"

—but she just smiled sweetly and went on to dispense to other guests' particular tastes without inquiring first.

I spotted Francesca in the group at the piano, so wandered on over remembering what she'd said earlier about a bite in her studio as she turned me down for dinner. All these folks were dressed in casual evening attire, no tuxes or ball gowns, but decidedly dressed up just a bit—Francesca quite a bit, in contrast to jeans and smock and bare feet. She wore a white sheath between knees and décolletage, high-heel pumps, sparkling earrings and necklace, hair upswept with flowers in it; looked downright edible.

I told her that, and she responded with a cold gaze and an aloof manner as she inquired, "Does that mean you're hungry or horny?"

I soberly replied, "Well, definitely not horny. Is this place heaven or hell? What's going on here?"

She said, still a bit haughty, "Heaven and hell both are mere states of mind, Ashton. I take it that Hai Tsu attended you well."

I said, "That's one way of putting it. How'd you know about that? Does she bathe and tell?"

Francesca was thawing. Her eyes sparkled a bit as she replied, "Very little escapes me here."

I sparkled back as I said, "Not even me."

She said, "Especially you, love."

Then she began introducing me to the others, given names only, and I remembered the dream on names and began tying attributes to the names given. On the male side there were John the Ascetic, Hilary the Fanatic, Pierre the Lunatic, and Karl the Magnificent; the females were Rosary the Devout and Catherine the Impudent. I was not introduced to the guy at the piano and could not see him very well behind the music stand although there was no music on it.

John was a logician, Hilary a priest, Pierre a chemist, Karl an engineer, Rosary a nun, and Catherine a whore—or so she said.

All seemed a trifle nutty, or perhaps just mysteriously shy. Whatever, they were good company and we were all laughing and talking together as we went in to dinner. A good-looking bunch for sure, all of them; prime of life, intelligent, witty. It turns out that they all live at Pointe House, and apparently have done so for quite some time.

John the Ascetic posed a trick syllogism over appetizers: "Major premise, all fire engines are red; minor premise, Russians are reds; therefore . . . ?"

Pierre the Lunatic flared his eyes as he declared, "The major premise is flawed. Not all fire engines are red."

"Used to be," insisted John. "So backdate the conclusion."

Karl the Magnificent guffawed and decided, "Therefore all firemen are communists."

"Excellent reasoning," congratulated Hilary the Fanatic.

"Not all communists are firemen!" squealed Catherine the Impudent, for another conclusion.

"Bravo!" said Hilary, applauding.

But John frowned and said, "No, no; that won't do. You must reason from the major to the minor to produce the conclusion."

Catherine screwed her face up and burst forth with another gleeful try: "All reds are great in bed!"

"No, no," John protested. "You don't have the right—"

"I like the way she does it," Hilary protested.

"Try it on your noble divinities, then," John suggested. "Major, All is God; minor, God is Love; therefore . . . ?"

"All is love," said Hilary quickly.

"Oh no, no no—you have to do it Catherine's way," John insisted.

She said brightly, "God is great in bed?"

"Jesus Christ!" said the priest.

"Him, too?" the whore asked, hopeful.

"I think I am going to throw up," said Rosary the Nun.

See? This is the cast of characters at Pointe House. The piano player did not come in to dinner, so I presumed that he was one of the shadow people like Hai Tsu and her helpers.

It was a most revealing dinner. We had escargot and artichokes, then vichyssoise and tough bread, later squab and mint jelly and something I was *told* was lamb fetus and fresh raw garden vegetables; after that sherbets and spumone and cannoli, then brandy and coffee—altogether a total debauchery of the taste buds and distender of intestinal boundaries. But the revelations came from the diners themselves. It was, as I said, a nutty bunch—but they were having fun, and I tumbled to the fact very quickly that these were brilliant personalities, one and all.

The piano player came in after dessert. He had brandy and a cigar with us. I learned later that he never ate with the others, but he was the most brilliant of all. He held me spellbound for twenty minutes while discussing the nature of nature with the chemist and the engineer, all the while playing at syllogisms with the logician and naughty repartee with the whore.

His name was Valentinius . . . or whatever. His friends just called him Val—and that was good enough for me too.

But I suspected that he was really St. Germain. And I was beginning to understand Valory's problems with names.

I doubt that I have ever had such a pleasant evening as that one at Pointe House. The conversations were both stimulating and enthralling and the range of interests was literally unbounded. We talked history and physics and art and politics, metaphysics and magic and human psychology, architecture and plumbing and ecology and geophysics, and on and on with one subject blending into another without pause or jumps—the theory of music drifting naturally into a discussion of *I Ching*, and that into Confucianism en route to cosmology and Indeterminancy, then back to Renaissance art and monarchy and classical philosophy and on and on.

The scope of wisdom displayed was always superior and often astonishing. These people were dropping names like Hollywood agents and inside info like congressional aides; like, "No no, Beethoven understood perfectly well that . . ."

"Of course the conflict with Robespierre was simply due to . . ."

"He couldn't have possibly understood plate tectonics. Good lord, even Newton thought . . ."

"Now Brahe, see . . . *that* one, see, would have made a fine court astrologer, but . . ."

"Of course they were not mad! Was Dali mad when he . . . ?"

Not sophomoric either—no pedantic posturing or empty displays of learning—these people were dissecting the meat and potatoes of life, and each was a chef with a surgeon's scalpel.

Later we gathered around the piano and sang while Val accompanied unobtrusively, after which he treated us to a solo concerto played as I had never heard it played before. Still later I watched breathlessly as Catherine danced and Rosary joined Val at the piano with a violin, followed by Karl with a comic Cossack interpretation of the Fire Dance, then Hilary and Francesca teamed up to show us what a waltz is really all about.

Never had I been so entertained, never so impressed by spontaneous performances, never before drawn so subjectively into an appreciation of artful talent.

And never so diverted from my own imperatives.

I suddenly realized that it was midnight and still I had not advanced my own understanding of the situation by one iota. We were saying our good-nights and I was trying to get to Valentinius.

But I did not find Valentinius and we did not say good-night or anything else in private. Everyone just drifted away and I found myself suddenly alone with Francesca.

She showed me a sympathetic smile, took my hand, and said to me, "Come along, my love, and I will show you what you need to know."

Not *tell* me; *show* me.

I'd been shown quite enough already, thanks.

But I allowed the beautiful lady to lead me to her studio. And there I discovered that I had not seen anything yet— nor had I learned anything yet about names and naming, life and death, echoes and omens.

What's in a name?

I was about to find out.

ELEVEN

Chronology

I warned you up front that this is a wild story and that I would not have known how to relate it to you until very recently. To merely lay out the events in chronological order, as I experienced them, would result not in a story but in a mere vignette of apparent fantasy—incomprehensible, unbelievable, unworthy of your serious attention. The chief problem, you see, is context. Any event occurring totally out of context with the circumstances that produce the event is likely to be incomprehensible—and something that is incomprehensible is also generally unbelievable and therefore fantastic.

Consider for example the birth of a child. It is an incomprehensible and seemingly magical event if totally disconnected from its context. Try to imagine a group of people isolated upon a small island who have been there since early childhood, the result of a shipwreck or air disaster or whatever. Somehow they have survived although they arrived there as babes and with no adult care or guidance. They are male and female and have matured sexually, so have mated instinctively without understanding the full significance of the act. Then one day a small human otherwise much like themselves emerges from one of the females. Magic? You bet it's magic, until the group begins relating effect to cause and comes up with a more rational understanding of the event. Moreover, if a small party had been exploring the other side of the island when that birth occurred—and a runner was dispatched to announce the miracle—that announcement would likely be met with disbelief and ridicule. A small stranger crawled from the tickle-place of Walks-in-Beauty? That's crazy! Who are you trying to kid!

I've got the same problem here, pal.

It's a context problem.

So I really need to talk a bit more about the context before you decide that I'm crazy or else I'm trying to kid you.

I need to go back to the St. Germain story because that is one of the contextual boundaries. Remember that I quoted the Countess d'Adhemar from her *Souvenirs de Marie Antoinette*, where she related a dangerous rendezvous with St. Germain during the intrigues of the French Revolution and his promise that she would see him "five times more."

You should be aware that this was during a period of great political upheaval and ambitious maneuvers, the early days of the First Republic. The young Napoleon was a junior army officer not yet into his stride toward empire, the French nation was at war within and also moving toward conflict with virtually all of Europe, and France was in chaos. The moment was prelude to the Reign of Terror, during which 300,000 Frenchmen were arrested, 17,000 executed, and many died in prison without trial. Robespierre was blamed for much of the "excess"—but all was excess in those days, and one man alone could not have done all that.

The New France rose from this tumult with Napoleon Bonaparte at the helm, but only after successive coups and bloody intrigues.

At the moment of St. Germain's rendezvous with the countess at a Parisian church, the French monarchy had been compromised and the nation was being governed by the National Convention, which was dominated by Robespierre. But four years earlier, Marie Antoinette had received prophetic warning from her "mysterious adviser," a man who had never revealed himself to her in person but who nonetheless had watched over the young queen since her entry into France, giving her counsel in the form of anonymous letters. Thus in 1788 she received a missive which she felt compelled to share with Countess d'Adhemar, and about which she was moved to confide: ". . . these are strange experiences. Who is this personage who has taken an interest in me for so many years without making himself known, without seeking any reward, and who yet has always told me the truth? He now warns me of the overthrow of everything that exists and, if he gives a gleam of hope, it is so distant that I may not reach it."

Handing the letter to the countess, the queen added,

"This time the oracle has used the language which becomes him; the epistle is in verse."

Countess d'Adhemar faithfully copied the verse into her diary:

The time is fast approaching when imprudent
   France,
Surrounded by misfortune she might have spared
   herself,
Will call to mind such hell as Dante painted.
This day, O Queen! is near, no more can doubt
   remain,
A hydra vile and cowardly, with his enormous
   horns
Will carry off the altar, throne, and Themis;
In place of common sense, madness incredible
Will reign, and all be lawful to the wicked.
Yea! Falling shall we see sceptre, censer, scales,
Towers and escutcheons, even the white flag;
Henceforth will all be fraud, murders and violence,
Which we shall find instead of sweet repose.
Great streams of blood are flowing in each town;
Sobs only do I hear, and exiles see!
On all sides civil discord loudly roars,
And uttering cries on all sides virtue flees,
As from the assembly votes of death arise.
Great God! who can reply to murderous judges?
And on what brows august I see the sword descend!
What monsters treated as the peers of heroes!
Oppressors, oppressed, victors, vanquished . . .

The storm reaches you all in turn, in this common
   wreck,
What crimes, what evils, what appalling guilt,
Menace the subjects, as the potentates!
And more than one usurper triumphs in command,
More than one heart misled is humbled and repents.
At last, closing the abyss and born from a black
   tomb
There rises a young lily, more happy, and more fair.

This prophecy, appalling as it was, was not heeded. Four years later, on the eve of her rendezvous with St. Germain, Countess d'Adhemar received the following note, in the same hand, and signed *Comte de St.-Germain*:

All is lost, Countess! This sun is the last which will set on the monarchy; tomorrow it will exist no more, chaos will prevail, anarchy unequalled. You know all I have tried to do to give affairs a different turn; I have been scorned; now it is too late . . . I will watch over you; be prudent, and you will survive the tempest that will have beaten down all. I resist the desire that I have to see you; what should we say to each other? You would ask of me the impossible; I can do nothing for the King, nothing for the Queen, nothing for the Royal Family, nothing even for the Duc d'Orleans, who will be triumphant tomorrow and who, all in due course, will cross the Capitol to be thrown from the top of the Tarpeian rock. Nevertheless, if you would care very much to meet with an old friend, go to the

eight o'clock Mass at the *Recollets*, and enter the
second chapel on the right hand.

How good a prophet was St. Germain? He was dead
center. His prophetic verse could be a capsule history of
time, foretold, and deadly accurate even in the most literal
sense. The revolution was actually a series of revolts and
power struggles between various contending factions, rag-
ing back and forth for years and seeing a steady succession
of leaders rising and toppling—and it was a revolt not
simply of the peasant against the crown but of class against
class, farmer versus urbanite, artisan versus businessman,
all versus the church in one form or another, the church
against all at various times, nobility undercutting nobility
and plotting against king or nation, king resisting all and
betraying the nation to its enemies without, military versus
militia and both ready to strike at any hand—more than ten
years toward the struggle for "liberty, equality, and frater-
nity" but culminating with the 18th Brumaire in military
dictatorship by the thirty-year-old general, Napoleon, who
became first emperor of France.

It was not until Napoleon's defeat by the European allies
in 1814 that the last line of St. Germain's prophecy began
to have meaning, because Napoleon was mere epilogue to
the French Revolution—or perhaps he was the vector;
whatever, the flowering of St. Germain's lily into the modern French Republic was still some time away.

But the year is now 1792; Louis XVI and his queen are
in the shadow of the guillotine and a mighty nation is beginning its descent into the abyss. A mysterious foreigner
known by many names has traveled to Paris in the name of

friendship to counsel the queen's endangered friend, who writes in her diary: "A cry of surprise escaped me; he still living, he who was said to have died in 1784, and whom I had not heard spoken of for long years past—he had suddenly reappeared, and at what a moment, what an epoch! Why had he come to France? Was he then never to have done with life? For I knew some old people who had seen him bearing the stamp of forty or fifty years of age, and that at the beginning of the 18th century!"

The Countess d'Adhemar had her meeting with St. Germain shortly before the king was seized and bound over for trial. And this is her record of that final conversation, quoted earlier in part:

"I have written it to you, *I can do nothing, my hands are tied by a sense stronger than myself*. There are periods of time when to retreat is impossible, others when *He* has pronounced and the decree will be executed. *Into this we are entering*."

"Will you see the Queen?"

"No, she is doomed."

"Doomed! To what?"

"To death."

Oh, this time I could not keep back a cry. I rose on my seat, my hands repulsed the Comte, and in a trembling voice I said:

"And you too! you! what, you too!" [Saying this.]

"Yes, I—I, like Cazotte."

"You know. . . ."

"What you do not even suspect. Return to the Palace, go and tell the Queen to take heed to herself, that this day will be fatal to her; there is a plot, murder is premeditated."

"You fill me with horror, but the Comte d'Estaing has promised . . ."

"He will take fright, and will hide himself."

"But M. de Lafayette . . ."

"A balloon puffed out with wind! Even now they are setting what to do with him, whether he shall be instrument or victim; by noon all will be decided. The hour of repose is past, and the decrees of Providence must be fulfilled."

"In plain words, what do they want?"

"The complete ruin of the Bourbons; they will expel them from all the thrones they occupy, and in less than a century they will return to the rank of simple private individuals in their different branches."

"And France?"

"Kingdom, Republic, Empire, mixed Governments, tormented, agitated, torn; from clever tyrants she will pass to others who are ambitious without merit. She will be divided, parcelled out, cut up; and these are no pleonasms that I use, the coming times will bring about the overthrow of the Empire; pride will sway or abolish distinctions, not from virtue but from vanity, and it is through vanity that they will come back to them. The French, like children playing with handcuffs and slings, will play with titles, honors, ribbons; everything will be a toy to them, even to the shoulder-belt of the National Guard [one of Napoleon's routes to power]; the greedy will devour the finances. Some fifty millions now form a deficit, in the name of which the Revolution is made. Well! under the dictatorship of the philanthropists, the rhetoricians, the fine talkers, the State debt will exceed several thousand millions!"

"You are a terrible prophet! When shall I see you again?"

"Five times more; do not wish for the sixth. Do not let me detain you longer. There is already disturbance in the city. I am like Athalie, *I wished to see and I have seen*. Now I will take up my part again and leave you. I have a journey to take to Sweden; a great crime is brewing there, I am going to try to prevent it. His Majesty Gustav III interests me, he is worth more than his renown."

"And he is menaced?"

"Yes; no longer will 'happy as a king' be said, and still less as a queen."

"Farewell, then, Monsieur; in truth I wish I had not listened to you."

"Thus it is ever with us truthful people; deceivers are welcomed, but fie upon whoever says that which will come to pass! Farewell, Madame; *au revoir*!"

This is not a story within a story.

This *is* the story.

You will understand why I say that when next you encounter the enchanting Francesca. And you will be a step ahead of me, pal, when I was there.

TWELVE

Series Earth

It was shortly past midnight when Francesca took me to her studio to show me what I needed to know. The entire room had been converted into a gallery to display her show of paintings and sculptures, and I realized instantly that my earlier exposure to her work had been to but a small sample of the whole. Wall, easel, and pedestal now displayed some forty to fifty striking portraits and an equal number of life-size sculpted heads.

The portraits were most arresting, in that the face of each subject seemed to have been caught by the eye of the artist just as it was emerging from a deeply dimensioned background of sheer color, each color blending into the other while overlaying somehow in a strangely translucent effect yet converging and mixing at the surface to produce the portrait.

I wondered how the hell she did that.

Each face was unique, yet . . . connected, somehow, to all the others—some commonality implied by expression or by some subtle handling of the eyes, or . . .

I had studied about five of those faces—very closely—when Francesca casually inquired, "What do you think?"

I replied without looking at her, "This is beautiful work. How do you get those colors to . . . mix in there like that?"

She replied, "The colors tell the story, do they not? Is all of art not representation?—and is all of representation not illusion?—and is all of illusion not allegory?"

I looked at her then as I said to her, "This is the show you've been developing."

"Yes."

"I seem to detect some theme to all of this."

"Yes. I call this *Series Earth*."

I said, "I see," but I did not see.

"Do you?"

"Not really. It's haunting, but I guess all good art is haunting." I was moving along the portraits more quickly, now. I told her, "I have seen all the others, but not Valentinius. Why no Valentinius?"

She replied mysteriously, "He is there."

I said, "Guess I missed him. Did you ever paint St. Germain?"

She gave me a perplexed look, averted her gaze for a long moment then brought it back to say, "I have been there, but . . ."

"I wasn't talking about a place."

"Oh. I referred to Saint-Germain-en-Laye, at the outskirts of Paris." She said it *Pah-ree*. "Some famous treaties were concluded there. Louis XIV built a chateau there, overlooking the Seine. A lovely spot. But I did not paint it."

"I was talking about Le Comte de St. Germain."

"There is no Le Comte de St. Germain."

"Used to be. I understand he befriended the French throne and particularly Marie Antoinette."

Those beautiful eyes rebounded instantly from mine and brimmed with moisture. "Dear heart," she murmured.

I felt suddenly very weird and awkward. Were we thinking of the same "let them eat cake" queen? "Yes," I said, not knowing what else to say.

"And so misunderstood. They hated her first because she was Austrian, then they hated her the more for fleeing that hatred and taking refuge at the bosom of kinder friends. The French, the French . . . they do not know how to treat a lady."

I said, "Always thought they revered their ladies."

She said, eyes still brimming with tears, "They revere prostitutes who masquerade as ladies. They burn or behead their ladies."

I had the strongest urge to take her in my arms and comfort her, but I just said, "Well, not in a long time."

She replied, "Once is quite enough."

I was thinking about the two Francescas. The one I had met first on arrival at Pointe House was your typical American girl-next-door. *This* Francesca was old-world European in both manner and language, and I was more than a little disturbed by that—much more so than by our conversation on the beach, earlier. I mean, after all, this is Southern California—Laguna Beach even, which has its cup overrunning with sects and ashrams—where one hardly blinks an eye anymore at hearing public references to past lives, mystic experiences, and the like. Such talk is part of the environment here; you do not feel compelled to interpret it literally.

I was disturbed also by the works of art; this stuff had *master* stamped all over it, yet I had never heard of Francesca Amalie before Pointe House, nor, I suspected, had the art world. Does an artist of this stature emerge overnight, with no shadows cast before her?

And the clay!—those beautifully sculpted heads that seemed ready to come to life at the snap of some magician's fingers . . .

I had to look again, and I was right: sculptures and paintings were all of a piece, went together, almost blended together—yet every lump of clay was Valentinius!

"He is there," she'd told me.

Damn right he was there.

He was there in each of them.

THIRTEEN

On the Beach

I was suddenly dog-tired in both mind and body—soul-weary maybe—so I said good-night to Francesca as soon as I could go gracefully, and went straight up to bed. I paid no attention to the time but it must have been close to one o'clock when I reached my suite. I stripped naked and got in bed, intending to mentally review the day's events, but I guess I was asleep before my head was firmly upon the pillow.

I slept well and did not dream of Pointe House, thank God. Hai Tsu awakened me at a few minutes past eight with coffee and juice on the side table. "Official visitor awaits, Shen," she informed me.

I guessed that she meant Jim Sloane, the lawyer, and I wanted to see him too, so I asked her to make him comfortable and to tell him that I would be right down.

I hit the shower as soon as Hai Tsu left the room, then got into tennis shorts, a polo shirt, and sneakers, and went down without shaving.

Sloane was not in the library and there was no sign of Hai Tsu so I went exploring and found the "official visitor" enjoying coffee at a courtyard table. Actually there were two visitors and neither was Jim Sloane. They were plain-clothes cops from the county of Orange, Sergeant Alvarez and Detective Beatty; they were being entertained by Francesca in skintight workout suit and nothing else—and obviously enjoying the experience immensely.

They stood up to shake my hand anyway as we exchanged introductions. I have worked with cops, but not much in this particular jurisdiction. These two seemed like nice guys, entirely courteous and affable, relaxed, respectful. Francesca I (the girl-next-door) laughed lightly as we all sat down. "Now you can tell me why you're here," she declared in a conspiratorial tone. "It's driving me crazy."

Alvarez and Beatty exchanged glances but both were smiling as Alvarez looked at me and said, "The house-keeper tells me that you two are the only residents."

I opened my mouth to correct that impression, then decided to save it for later. The cop did not notice; he was already asking, "Who drives the Maserati?"

I said, "Guilty."

He turned the gaze to Francesca, asked, "And the VW Beetle . . . ?"

"Mine all mine," she said. "Made the last payment two months ago, so you couldn't be here to repossess it."

"No other vehicles on the property," the cop noted.

"Only when someone comes," she replied.

I said, "Uh, I am one of those someones. I don't live here."

The two cops again exchanged glances. Beatty took a sip of his coffee and Alvarez asked me, "Where do you live, Mr. Ford?"

"I live in Malibu."

"Would you mind telling me why you spent the night here last night?"

I replied, "Not after you've told me why you want to know."

He smiled, said, "We are conducting a routine investigation. You are not suspected or accused of any crime. We'd appreciate it if you would cooperate, make our job simple, and we can be on our way without disturbing you further."

I asked, "Routine investigation of what?"

He sighed, glanced at Beatty, said, "The air patrol spotted a body on the beach below this house early this morning. We are trying to develop information relative to that."

I said, "I'll bet you are. Are we talking a *dead* body?"

"Yes. Male. Fully clothed. Apparently fell from the top of the cliff. The body had not been in the water."

Francesca was holding her breath, staring at the cop and hanging on every word. She softly exclaimed, "Wow! This is a *murder* investigation!"

Alvarez showed her a faintly embarrassed smile as he replied, "Not at all. Cause of death has not been determined. We are merely developing information. Your housekeeper assured us that no one here is missing. So—"

I asked, "Have you identified the victim?"

"No. It's the body of a white male, age thirty to thirty-five, no identification."

I lit a cigarette, pushed back my chair, said, "I arrived from Malibu at about two o'clock yesterday afternoon and had a meeting with Jim Sloane of Sloane, Sloane and James, attorneys for the owner of this property. I have been retained to develop information, to use your own terminology, for use in the defense of a suit by the state of California to seize this property. That is all I know about anything here. But of course I will cooperate with your investigation in any way that I can."

Beatty had been taking notes as I spoke.

Alvarez smiled and told me, "Thanks, we appreciate your attitude. You wouldn't mind taking a look at the body, then, and . . ."

"How did you recover it?"

"Still there. One of our marine units from Newport Harbor is on the scene and standing by. And of course we'd appreciate it if our medical examiners could use your private access to, uh, reach and secure the scene. They should be here at most any minute now. I'm assuming that you do have beach access. We noted stairs from the lower shelf. Do they go—?"

"To an elevator," I told him. "Entry hall, inside the house."

"No other way down?"

I said, "Sounds like someone found it."

He gave me a wry smile, said, "Could we see the elevator?"

The guy wanted to see more than the elevator, so I

played his game and led them through the long way so he could satisfy his curiosity inside. Hell, I just took charge, assuming it was expected of me by whoever sent for me. We encountered Hai Tsu along the way. I explained the situation to her and hinted that it could be a long day of official traipsings. I have to say that I was a bit numb about the entire thing; the news of a corpse on the beach neither alarmed nor surprised me. But I did suggest that she contact Sloane and alert him to the situation.

As it worked out, Francesca and I took the elevator down with Alvarez; Beatty remained topside to greet and direct the expected official traffic.

A powerful looking police cruiser was idling just beyond the surf line and two deputies in wet suits were on the beach. They'd covered the body with an orange tarp and were just sitting there on the sand as though enjoying a day at the beach. Alvarez excused himself and went over to have a word with them.

Francesca seemed fascinated by the orange tarp.

She murmured, "Who in the world could it be? How could he get here?"

I looked up, straight up along the cliff above the body, and saw the roof of Pointe House—and then I began to lose the numbness. This was *my side* of the house; the windows of my suite were directly above. There was only one way that body could have gotten there—and I was sure that fact had not been lost on Alvarez.

Developing information, my ass.

Francesca had been right on. This was a murder investigation.

And guess who all the prime suspects must be. One real live man, maybe, and a houseful of ghosts, maybe. So where did that leave good old Ashton?

Exactly. Exactly.

I could hardly wait to see that body.

FOURTEEN

Deathline

The body of Jim Sloane was beneath that tarp. It lay face up, eyes open, lips pulled back in a frozen snarl or grimace, dressed as I had last seen him; rather badly broken up by the apparent fall, limbs at grotesque angles. The corpse struck no apparent note of recognition within Francesca; she merely shuddered and quickly turned away.

I knelt beside the body for a closer look, then told Sergeant Alvarez, "It's Jim Sloane, the lawyer I met here yesterday. Looks like the same clothing."

"Did you see him leave the property after that meeting?"

"No. But I was down here myself from five o'clock till about six. So was Francesca. We couldn't have missed him if he'd been here at that time."

Francesca was looking at me oddly.

Alvarez quietly stated, "I'm guessing no more than

twelve hours dead. Did you see or hear anything out of the ordinary during the night?"

I'd seen and heard plenty out of the ordinary but I did not intend to go into any of that with this guy. "If you mean a commotion or outcry, no."

"What did you do with your evening?"

I resisted the temptation to sneak a look at Francesca, told him, "Took a bath and a nap before dinner. Dined with Miss Amalie. We spent the evening talking and . . . getting to know each other. I previewed her upcoming art show at about midnight, then went straight to bed. I was still in bed when you got here."

I should have checked with Francesca first.

She was plainly aghast at what I'd said; stepped closer to Alvarez and murmured, "That's not true."

The cop gave her a reassuring look; gave me a hard one as he told me, "That's in conflict with Miss Amalie's earlier statement. She has said that she last saw you at approximately six o'clock yesterday evening."

I muttered, "Then we've got a problem here, haven't we."

The coroner's man arrived at that juncture, postponing the problem to another moment.

Francesca was getting the shakes. Alvarez excused her to return to the house but it was obvious that he was not extending the same courtesy to me. I retreated to a rock and sat there in dark thought while the homicide team did their number; then Alvarez collected me and we returned topside together.

On the way up I told him, "I'd appreciate it if you'd make a call on my behalf as soon as we get to the house—

Lieutentant Paul Steward, Homicide, LAPD." I found a card in my wallet and handed it to him. "We've worked together in the past. He knows me and knows what I do. All I'm asking is that you talk to him before you talk to me. Because frankly, pal, we've got a mind-boggler here, and there's no way I can bring it home for you unless you're willing to at least fairly consider what I have to tell you."

The sergeant made no comment to that, but he accepted Stewart's card and went straight to a telephone as soon as we were inside the house. He spoke with the L.A. homicide detective for several minutes, looking me up and down from time to time, and his manner was a bit warmer —though still reserved—when he returned to me.

"I never worked with a psychic," he told me. "Not sure I really buy any of it. Anyway, that's not the issue. Stewart says he'd cock his pistol and hand it to you in a dark alley, he's that trustful of you. That buys you nothing here of course, if you turn up smudgy. And I will not hand you my cocked pistol—not here, now, or anywhere. But I'll give you some space, for the time being. What did you want to tell me?"

I replied, "First of all, I believe that Miss Amalie thinks she is telling the truth about last night. I cannot speak for the housekeeper—what she does or does not believe—but I can tell you that she misled you about the number of people who are staying here. There are at least five and possibly six others besides Miss Amalie and myself, who dined formally here last night and who gave every appearance of having resided here for a long time—much longer, I'm sure, than you would care to believe."

"You are saying that she—Miss Amalie—attended a formal dinner party here last night?"

"Yes."

"She told me that she had a sandwich and a Coke for dinner in her studio, and worked until midnight."

I replied, "She may believe that she's telling the truth."

"What does that mean? Could she be in two places at once?"

I said, "It is not impossible."

"I am trying to be patient with you," the cop said darkly.

I said, "Please keep trying, because you haven't heard anything yet."

He said, "Then let's save it for now. I'd like to see your room."

So I led him upstairs, ushered him into my suite, lit a cigarette, and watched him violate my civil rights. He looked in every closet, drawer, nook, and cranny—and when he was finished, he asked me, "Do you still maintain that you are not living here?"

I told him, "I saw this place for the first time yesterday afternoon."

He asked, "Do you always travel so heavy? Isn't all this stuff yours?"

I replied, "No, it is not mine. I came here with an overnight kit, not even sure I'd be staying the night. Found everything exactly as you see it." I tugged at my polo shirt. "This too. I came down here in slacks and blazer. They picked up some sand on the beach, so—"

"Where are they now?"

I went to the closet and searched vainly, turned back to tell the cop, "Guess Hai Tsu picked them up for cleaning.

Look at all this other stuff closely though, you'll see it's all brand new. I can tell you that it all fits and that it is the kind of stuff I usually wear, depending on the occasion."

"But it was just sitting waiting for you when you arrived, not knowing that you would even stay the night?"

"That's right. The computer is loaded with my software too. It appears that every effort was exerted to make me feel at home."

Alvarez looked around, commented, "Beats hell out of mine."

I said, "Mine too."

He went to the large window in the bedroom, slid it open, leaned out—stayed out there twenty or so seconds —pulled his head back inside and beckoned to me. "Come see," he said quietly.

I went, and I saw. It was a clean drop to the beach below, to the very spot where the corpse had lain and now marked by an outline in the sand.

I said, "Yeah, I had that figured out from below."

He said, "Me too. Had this window already staked out."

I told him, "I can't explain it yet. But I was absent from this suite from about eight o'clock until almost one. I was—"

"Dining with Miss Amalie."

"That's right, plus six others. Well, five others during dinner. St. Germain never eats with other people so . . ." I realized too late what I was saying, tried to cover it, failed.

The cop said, "Who is St. Germain?"

I said, "Inside joke. His real name is Valentinius de

Medici. He owns the joint. But I gather that he doesn't stay here all the time. Sort of a world traveler you might say."

"Uh huh. The housekeeper didn't mention him."

I said, "That doesn't surprise me. She didn't mention the others either, did she."

He produced a notebook, glanced at it, told me, "Household staff of three, including her; two gardeners and a general maintenance man live in the cottage in the garden area—all Chinese, no English spoken; you, and Miss Amalie. No mention of a—how do you spell that?"

I found my overnight kit, produced the two bundles of money wrapped in the power of attorney, placed the package in Alvarez's hands, told him, "Note the date on the document. The ten grand was dropped on me at Malibu. Sloane delivered the power of attorney after I got here yesterday. Why would I push the man out my window? I had just been hired—or let's say *retained* to work with him in an effort to save this property from confiscation by the state."

The cop was examining the bundles. He looked up to say, "So you'd met with this Medici before you came down from Malibu."

"In a manner of speaking, yes."

"What does that mean?"

"It means that he dropped the money on me and asked me to come immediately."

"So the two of you came—?"

"No, he just dropped the money and the summons, then disappeared. I came on—"

"How disappeared?"

"Same way he appeared. Blip, he's in. Blip, he's out."

"I'm not sure I understand. . . ."

"Don't try, not yet. I don't understand it either yet."

"You sound like you think you will though."

"I usually manage to, sooner or later. This one may be more later than sooner, so don't hold your breath. I—"

"Wouldn't think of it. Who were the other people at dinner?"

I gave him a long, quiet look, then told him, "You really don't want to know, not yet."

"Try me," the cop invited.

I said, "Well, let's see—we had John the Ascetic—he poses syllogisms, and—"

"Poses what?"

"Syllogisms. It's a propositional form of deductive logic—the kind of games cops play—"Elementary, my dear Watson," that kind. Only John's are done for fun; you're supposed to come up with comic examples of flawed logic."

"Okay. Who else?"

"Hilary the Fanatic—some sort of priest—I don't know, maybe a Jesuit. Rosary the Devout—a nun, but I don't know which order; her habit looks like it came from medieval times. Pierre the Lunatic—chemist, he says, but I think alchemist. Karl the Magnificent is an engineer; I get it that he specializes in feats, like Notre Dame and the Eiffel Tower or maybe even pyramids—who knows? Last but certainly not least, we have Catherine the Impudent, who insists that she's a whore but I think may still be a virgin. Did I give you six?"

Alvarez was standing near the doorway with notebook in hand and pencil poised but unmoving, his mouth open, gazing at me with the look of a highly intelligent man who wonders if he is being double-talked.

He put the notebook away and pocketed the pencil, turned toward the open door and said, without looking at me, "What is this lawsuit? On what grounds is the state confiscating?"

"They contend that the legal owner of record would now have to be at least 150 years old, that obviously he has died intestate and without heirs."

"So what about Medici? Can't he produce——?"

"He is that legal owner of record."

"You mean . . . ?"

"Uh huh."

Alvarez went on to the door, then turned back to look in my general direction but not directly at me, said, "Stewart recommended that I give you space to operate. Okay, but that does not mean space to bamboozle. Don't leave the property without notifying me first."

I replied, "Thanks. How much time does that space buy me?"

"Not much," he said, shifting his gaze to meet my own. "Just till I can unscramble things a bit. Be advised; you are a suspect at least until I can do that."

I requested, "Give me a time frame."

He replied, "How can I do that? But let's say twenty-four hours. I could book you right now, just on the face of things. But I've known Paul Stewart too for a long time.

So I'm giving you that much space. Don't make me regret it."

That kind of space was like a finger snap in time. But I had to be grateful, considering the circumstances, for all small favors received.

And it now appeared that I had a new deadline—or was it a *death*line? My ten days to resolution had shrunk to one.

FIFTEEN

The Power

Before he left, Sgt. Alvarez admitted that he'd known the identity of the victim all along. Sloane's wallet with everything intact had been found on the body. His car had been discovered illegally parked on Pacific Coast Highway just down from the entrance to Pointe House, which was something of a puzzler unless you wanted to think that (a) he had returned at some time following the afternoon visit and, for some reason, had wanted to enter unnoticed; or (b) someone else had parked the car on the highway, probably after Sloane's death.

Also I gained a modification of my stay put order from Alvarez; he agreed that I could travel freely within Orange County but that I should keep his office informed of my whereabouts.

I got Hai Tsu on the house phone as soon as the cops

had cleared out, asked her to come to my suite. She must have thought I desired valet attentions because she took one look at the stubble on my face and went to the bathroom for shaving gear. I needed a shave, sure, so I figured what the hell and let her go at it.

Always gives me a funny feeling to have someone else at my face and throat with a blade. But I tried to relax and enjoy it, thought I could use the shave as a cover for some pointed conversation. That did not work though. Every time I tried to frame a word in the mouth, Hai Tsu gently but quickly shut it off with a finger at my lips as if to say "no talking during shaving, please." I had no desire to lose chunks of nose or lip so I took the advice and held my silence until she'd finished.

Best damned shave I'd ever had. She kept me under warm towels for a minute or so afterward, then finished off by massaging a cooling balm into the skin.

"Breakfast now, Shen?" she inquired happily, as though that would really make her day.

I was hungry, yeah, but it could wait. I asked her, "Can you read English?"

She jerked her head in an enthusiastic nod, replied, "Oh yes, read English good. Hai Tsu read for Shen?"

I handed her the power of attorney and said, "Hai Tsu read for Hai Tsu."

If indeed she read that paper then she is the fastest speed-reader I've ever seen at work. She merely glanced at it and handed it back.

"Yes, Shen?"

"Read it."

"Yes, Shen." As though to say, "How many times, dummy?"

I asked, "You read it?"

"Yes, Shen."

"Then tell me about it."

"Is confirmation. Shen is here when not here."

Wait a minute! I was getting a whole new slant on that piece of paper!

I said, "It authorizes me to sign his name on legal documents."

She said, "Yes. And also act, be, do in every way as though Shen is in your body."

I was getting the *Shen* now too.

And the full *Shen* treatment!

"No, wait," I protested lamely, "a power of attorney is used to . . ."

After a moment of respectful waiting for me to finish the thought, Hai Tsu finished it for me in her own way. "You are Shen."

So I thought, well okay, what the hell, why not.

"Thanks," I muttered. "I'll, uh, be down in about ten minutes. Breakfast outside is fine. Two eggs medium, bacon if you have it."

"English muffins." She twinkled at me—confirming, not inquiring.

I replied, "Yes, crisp and dripping," but I knew she already knew that too, somehow.

I let her get to the door before I called her back and asked her, "How well did you know Sloane?"

"This Sloane, not know," she replied.

"You saw him yesterday for the first time?"

"First time, yes."

"You knew his father?"

"Yes. Many year."

I looked at that bright, beautiful face and wondered how it could have known anything at all for "many year" unless it began in childhood.

I wanted to push the thought a bit further. "And his father's father?"

"Yes, Shen."

Well damn it.

"How did you guys work this? I mean, did the Sloanes do all the banking and other financial matters? Where do you get your household money?"

"All is provided, Shen," is all she was prepared to tell me about that.

I knew that further questioning in this vein would not advance me beyond that blank wall, so I just dropped it for the moment and let the beautiful Oriental enigma go on her way.

Which does not mean that I did not have a thousand or so questions awaiting answers. The whole thing had taken a decidedly ominous twist—from the mysterious to the macabre maybe—and I was feeling entirely uncomfortable about a lot of things, the power of attorney among them.

Like, what the hell good was a power of attorney for a man who should be dead these hundred or more years? Death wipes away that power. So how did Valentinius—if I knew what I thought I knew—intend that I use it?

I thought of something he'd said to me at Malibu: "You are the man for me, Ashton."

The man to do what?

Hai Tsu told me, "You are Shen."

Bull *shit* I was Shen!

I was Ashton Ford, thank you, and intended to stay that way. But, as I looked around me at that fabulous master suite loaded with everything I could need or want in a home, I knew and realized and understood that—for the moment anyway—I was also Valentinius de Medici.

And that understanding shivered my bones.

What's in a name?

For the moment, pal . . . me.

The law offices of Sloane, Sloane and James occupied the musty second floor of an old office building in Santa Ana, the county seat. The partners had evidently found no need to put on a successful face. The furnishings, though entirely adequate and functional, looked as old as the building. The only modern touches were a small personal computer and a copy machine sharing a cubbyhole with Mr. Coffee and his accessories.

The lady at the reception desk looked like she'd come with the furniture, but she was sweet and hospitable—insisting that I wait with coffee for my audience with Claire Kelly, the legal secretary and office manager.

Ms. Kelly was about seventy too, and obviously ran the joint. I think she'd been in the john when I arrived, because she came in from the hallway while I was on my second coffee and took care to replace a fobbed key on a hook behind her desk, after which the reception sweetie glanced my way and announced, "Mr. *Ford* is here to visit, Claire."

Mr. Ford sloshed his coffee onto his slacks while preparing to meet Claire's enthusiastic charge-in-greeting. She cried, "Oh dear!" and went to work on the damage with a paper towel despite my insistence that it was okay. I think she made it worse, but I agreed with her when finally she decided, "There, that's better. You must never let a coffee stain set, you know."

It took a minute or two to get around the inauspicious beginning, to get me properly and comfortably seated at her desk, and to get her composed at the business side and glowing at me in expectation of who knows what. She was a sweet lady.

She said, "Well! Did you have a nice conference with Mr. Sloane?"

"Yes, I—"

"Everything in order?"

"Perfect order," I assured her. "I want—"

"It was such a shock but also such a pleasure to see Mr. de Medici yesterday! I cannot get over that man. I was telling Eunice, he hasn't changed a bit since the first time I saw him, and that must have been . . . my goodness, all of thirty years ago!"

I smiled and said, "Yes, amazing man."

"You tell him I want the name of his plastic surgeon."

We laughed.

I said, "Have you heard from Jim today?"

She sobered as she replied, "No, he hasn't come in yet." She glanced disapprovingly at the clock. "Not that I should be surprised. Did you have an appointment?"

Sometimes I lie, when the cause is right.

I told her, "Sort of informally. I told him I wanted to

drop by and get a copy of the file. Perhaps I misunderstood; I thought he would be here too..."

She waved a hand and set that matter straight. "That would depend on his golf schedule. No need for you to wait one minute, Mr. Ford, unless you just wish to discuss birdies and pars and whatever it is they do with those little balls. Jimmy would not know where to find the file anyway. Since his father..."

I ventured into what I perceived as a sore spot. "Well, he's still young. Maybe he'll take hold and surprise you one of these days. What about the other partner? Doesn't he...?"

"Well no, poor Mr. James has been an invalid for more than five years now. He is still in the firm, but only nominally."

I grinned as I asked her, "You don't play golf with Jimmy, eh?"

She replied, "Goodness, I wouldn't even know how to drive one of those dumb little carts they zoom about in."

Ms. Kelly excused herself and went into another room, reappeared a moment later with a legal folder tucked beneath an arm, took it to the copy machine.

The other lady—Eunice I presumed—informed me, "Mr. Thomas Sloane was a very good golfer too. It's all his fault if Jimmy tries to run his practice from the golf course. That boy was raised at the country club."

I shrugged and said, "Must be nice."

She said, "Well... we really have a very limited practice. Mr. de Medici's retainer rather dictates that."

Interesting idea. I said, "Dictates what?"

"I hope I haven't spoken out of turn. I assumed that you knew..."

I said, "Oh, yes, the limitation."

"And, after all, how many people around here need legal specialists in estates and trusts?"

I smiled and said, "That's right."

"But we keep busy enough," she added brightly.

I looked at my hands and wondered what the hell it was all about.

"Where is Thomas Sloane now?" I inquired.

"He's at Windmere Hill."

Sounded like a convalescent hospital. I let it rest right there, knowing that I could track it down if necessary.

Ms. Kelly completed her chore at the copier. She brought me a duplicate file, all properly assembled and bound into a legal folder, placed it in my hands. I had produced identification for neither of these ladies. They took me at my word and face. And of course I'd been giving them a bit of help at the subliminal level; no doubt they would not otherwise have been so trusting and open with even a familiar client.

Ms. Kelly accepted another mental cue to tell me, "No, dear me, I'm afraid I couldn't keep up, on a golf course. Jimmy usually plays with his college friend, Henry."

It tumbled right out of a flaring synapse: "You mean Hank...Hank Gibson."

"Yes. Nice boy. And a bit more ambitious than Jimmy, I'm sure."

I said, "I thought they'd had a falling-out."

"At least once a week," Ms. Kelly said smilingly. "But it doesn't interfere with their golf game."

Maybe it had, this week.

But I did not wish to be the one to break the news to these dear ladies.

I tucked the Medici file beneath a fevered arm and got the hell away from there before someone else could do so.

But I had not really "stolen" anything, you know.

Hell. I had the power.

SIXTEEN

Goose Eggs

The de Medici file was very interesting, even if not entirely enlightening. It was compartmentalized under subfiles labeled the Retainer, the Grant, the Estate, and Transactions.

The Retainer subfile contained a ruling document dated November 18th, 1918. It empowered Arthur J. Sloane, an attorney, to conduct business relative to the preservation of certain real estate "and ancillary interests" on behalf of Valentinius de Medici. It had a provision for "successors in interest" to ensure long-term application, and contained a "covenant" to the effect that Sloane and/or his successors would restrict their legal practice as a condition of the retainer. Apparently Valentinius had wanted assurance that his own interests would not become suffocated under competing interests within the firm—and he was willing to pay well for the exclusivity. The annual fee for services was stated as "an amount equal to seven-and-one-half percent of the latest assessed value of the estate."

Go figure it. Seven and a half percent of a million dollars is $75,000. Multiply that result by twenty or thirty—the modern value of the estate—and it is not difficult to understand why a law firm would gladly bind itself to a single client.

What was not readily understandable was why—with such a beautiful deal for the lawyers—they had allowed the golden goose to become so legally endangered. I mean, all they had to do with their lives was protect the estate that was enriching them. Why had they not done so?

. The Grant subfile offered a possible clue. It contained the legal language necessary to empower the attorneys for specific activities and to specifically exclude them from others. For example they could disburse moneys for routine maintenance and upkeep but could not authorize alterations or modifications on their own. Another restriction had to do with—"in no wise . . . undertake, implement, conduct, encourage or support any legal proceeding which would have the effect of"—changing legal ownership of the property.

I did not have the luxury of time required to sit down and analyze the several documents of that subfile—all in heavy legalese—but it was fairly apparent from just a light scan that Valentinius had screwed it down rather tightly.

The Estate subfile contained the documents shown to me earlier by Jim Sloane—also architectural abstracts for the rebuilding of Pointe House in 1921 and subsequent remodelings and renovations across the years.

The Transactions section brought a quiver or two. It was

a detailed ledger of money flow from Swiss numbered accounts to an international bank in Newport Beach, and there were several entries per year from 1918 to the present. The latest entry was several months old and reflected a transfer of $3.2 million into the Newport Beach account; a related subentry diverted 2.25 million of that to Sloane, Sloane and James for "annual retainer."

Two and a quarter million per year sounds like something worth fighting for, doesn't it. Or stealing for?

Put it together. Seven and a half percent per year gives you an amount equal to the whole thing every thirteen years or so. So Sloane, Sloane and James had, in effect, rolled it over five times already—and were still sitting astride that golden goose. Forget what Pointe House may be worth on the open market; it was worth far more as a *producer* of wealth for its custodians. How would you put a fair market value on something like that? If you had custody of the goose and someone approached you with the intention of buying your right to the annual fee—how much would you sell it for?

Of course they had not been receiving two and a quarter million each year since 1918. Their fee rose as property values in general rose—but it is all the same in the relative sense. If a hundred grand would have bought the property in 1918, then seven and a half percent of that in 1918 would buy you the same thing that the same percentage of the current market value would buy you today.

More to the point though: why was it that important to Valentinius?—so important that he was willing to pay such disproportionate fees for custodial care?

It was a question not to preoccupy the mind at that

point, but to be tucked away for future consideration. I had other bases to cover and not much time left in the game, so I set my sights for Newport Beach. Henry Gibson's Realty Holdings International Corp. was officed there, and Windmere Hill was situated in adjacent Costa Mesa.

It has been said, and I am willing to believe it, that Newport Beach is the financial capital of the West. It has a population under 100,000 and stands a full hour south of the Los Angeles Civic Center, but it is a business stronghold of immense diversity and is said to house more corporate power per square foot than any U.S. city. Much of that is grouped upon a hillside overlooking the Pacific in a business complex known as the Newport Center.

If California should one day tumble into the sea, as various prophets and soothsayers have predicted, then Newport Center will probably become the new Atlantis to be discovered and explored by some distant generation as a lesson in twentieth-century civilization, to be marveled at in its watery grave and to provoke endless discussions as to the significance of the architecture and the mysteries of the life-styles suggested by the ruins—the various temples and palaces, expansive promenades and courtyards, the bazaar and the wide, curving boulevards and immense stone and glass structures soaring into the sky. They probably will not get it right, but all will agree that this new Atlantis was an important cultural center of twentieth-century mankind.

And so it is.

The monolithic structure that housed the international bank through which Valentinius moved his funds also provided corporate home for Gibson's Reality Holdings. I stopped at the bank first and presented my credentials to a delighted vice-president who unfurled the red carpet for me and happily presented the accounts for my scrutiny. Accounts, yeah, two of them—one a sort of general fund accessible by Sloane, Sloane and James, with a current balance of $432,816.32—the other a household account under the care of one Ming Hai Tsu containing $37,280.90.

I transferred $400,000 from the general fund to the household account. The banker seemed a bit nervous about that, but what the hell could he do? I had the power. I took a transcript covering the past twelve months' activity in both accounts, thanked the guy for his efficiency, and went on to Gibson's offices.

Something was going on there; I could feel it in the air—a sort of electrical tingling that sensitive people can sometimes pick up on—some sort of mental energy I believe. Whatever, I experienced it even before I ventured through the double glass doors that admit you to this superswank alter ego of Sloane, Sloane and James. It must have cost the guy more per month than the law firm paid all year to present themselves to the public. From the gilt lettering on the doors to the space-age stylings inside, surrounding in splendor the yuppie receptionist who at least presented the suggestion of MBA, the entire gestalt reeked of moneyed success and undeniable position on the business ladder.

The receptionist was about twenty-five. She had square shoulders and a stiff upper lip, an easy smile that came maybe too easy at the surface with no involvement below; if there is a magazine for young upwardly mobile career women, she could qualify for the cover.

I told her I had a golf date with Hank—so where the hell was he.

She had me dissected and analyzed even before I opened my mouth. She gave me one of those quick surface movements of the lips—okay, call it a smile—and said, "I'm sorry . . . you are mister . . . ?"

"Ford," I said.

"Of course," she said and reached for the intercom.

I retreated to a neutral corner, still wondering how I wanted to play it when or if Gibson did or did not invite me in.

Didn't have long to wait.

A door opened behind the receptionist and Sergeant Alvarez leaned through.

He said, "Ford, what the hell!"

"Small world," I said, my throat suddenly gone almost too dry to speak.

"Small you ain't seen yet," he assured me. "Get in here!"

So I went in there.

The room was full of cops. I guess both Newport Beach and county cops—a coroner's homicide team and all that implies.

A guy about my age sat in a high-backed swivel chair behind a massive desk containing all sorts of hi-tech gadgets of the modern business world. He was blond, well built, handsome.

Well, call it exhandsome.

The guy was dead, lips stretched back in a familiar grimace, eyes open, body stiffly upright in advanced rigor mortis.

"Gibson?" I asked Alvarez.

"You bought it," he said.

Hell, I hadn't bought anything. Not even golden eggs from the prize goose.

But I had to wonder what the hell was buying me.

SEVENTEEN

The Elect

Alvarez himself had discovered this corpse. An appointment diary found on Sloane's body recorded a planned meeting with Gibson on the evening that Sloane died. Routinely checking that connection, Alvarez called on Gibson at his office and was told by the receptionist that her boss had not come in yet.

This was past eleven o'clock.

Alvarez had one of those cop quivers probably, and insisted on being shown into Gibson's private office.

In defense of the receptionist, who later stated that indeed she had looked inside that office earlier, the presence of a corpse was not that obvious when Alvarez first stepped inside. The swivel chair is high-backed, and it was turned sort of toward the windows; the angle of view from the doorway was such that you saw only the back of the chair at casual glance. So if the young lady had looked into that office earlier, then the discovery hours later that her boss had been sitting there dead all the while must have been an unnerving experience, to say the least. I sent her a mental apology for my initial reaction to her executive style; she was doing very well under the circumstances.

Alvarez was of course stretching the protocol on city turf by his very presence there, so he called it in to the Newport Beach police and stepped aside for them to handle it, though remaining to assist in view of the possibly related death at Laguna Beach.

There were no obvious wounds or signs of violence on this body. It looked as though the guy had just been sitting there at his desk, had some sort of seizure, and died.

"But look at the face," Alvarez unnecessarily added. "Same as the other guy. What is that?—terror or what?"

I said, "Yeah ... or pain, rage ... whatever, death abruptly stopped it."

He pulled me aside and lowered his voice to ask me, "So what brings the psychic detective to this latest scene of death?"

This was somewhat embarrassing. I had not deliberately withheld the information regarding Gibson's interest in Pointe House and Sloane's apparent animosity toward the guy; with all the other mystery, and the shock of finding myself a possible murder suspect, I simply had not thought to tell Alvarez about it. Now I tried to gloss it with vagueness. I told him, "Sloane mentioned this guy when he was briefing me on the legal problem. Seems that Gibson had been trying to broker a deal for some developer before the state stepped in with their claim. But that was the only connection I had until about an hour ago. Now it seems that these two were old college chums and still get together frequently on the golf course."

Alvarez said, "Uh huh. Where'd you get this?"

"Sloane's office."

"Why didn't you bring it to me then?"

"Would have," I said, "if something had turned. You and I are not working the same end of the stick, you know. You're investigating a suspicious death. I have been retained to prevent a confiscation of the estate. I guess that's what I'm expected to do. So—"

"What d'you mean, *guess*?"

"Just that. The guy just dropped the money on me and told me to get my ass down here on the double quick. He said there was a crisis that had to be resolved within ten days. Then Sloane comes over and lays this power of attorney on me. He is as baffled as I am. He's looking to me for answers; I'm looking to him for answers. All he knows is that the state will prevail on their claim unless he can produce a legal owner within ten days. So I put the ten days together and decide that this must be the crisis that Valentinius mentioned."

The cop had been giving me careful attention during that spiel. Now he fixed me with a fish-eye and asked, "What exactly did this Valentinius tell you?"

"You want total recall?"

"That would be nice."

"I am not here by error, Ashton. You are—"

"What's that?"

"You said total recall."

"Oh. Okay. Go ahead."

"You are the man for me. Let me assure you that you shall enjoy the assignment. A very beautiful woman is involved. And, of course, the pay is good. I understand that your usual fee is five hundred dollars per day. I offer you this, for ten days' services maximum. The job defines itself. Go to Laguna Beach. Contact Francesca Amalie. You shall find her at Pointe House. You must go today. The crisis is now. Help her to resolve it. Ten days maximum, or all is lost."

Alvarez was listening attentively. He waited a couple of beats after I'd finished, then said, "And . . . ?"

"That's it," I replied. "That's all he said to me."

"That's all he said."

"That's right."

"So on the basis of that—no more than that—you dropped everything and rushed down to Laguna?"

I said, "Well . . . that's all he *said*, but . . ."

"But what?"

"It was the way he said it. The way he looked. The way he appeared and disappeared. I don't fight the angels, pal."

"You assumed this was an *angel*?"

I shrugged. "How many humans have materialized and dematerialized in your presence?"

He was still giving me the fish-eye. "But you assumed *angel*. Why not *devil*?"

I said, "I've never met the devil."

He said, "But of course you have met angels."

I said, "Sure . . . frequently. It's a rather common experience."

"Wings and halos and the whole bit, huh?"

I explained, "Wings and halos are no more than artistic

representation of certain angelic attributes; that is, the ability to move freely through the air without machinery, and the body of light."

"Body of what?"

"Light. The light body. Also referred to as the astral body, the ethereal body, the spiritual body."

"But this guy Valentinius . . ."

"Some angels can materialize very dense bodies, much like yours and mine. You'd never know you were talking to an angel. Or—"

"Or what?"

I said, "Or making love to one."

He grinned. "Come on!"

I said, "It happens."

The grin broadened. "Maybe I had one the other night. How can you tell for sure?"

I replied—just joking, really, "Thrice is nice but there are seven levels to heaven."

He took it seriously. "Yeah?"

So I took it on. "Sure. The seventh heaven is orgasmic infinity."

Then I chuckled, and he chuckled, and the ice between us was broken forever. He said, "Fix me up sometime."

I said, "Sure."

"How d'you do that total recall thing? Is that for real?"

"It's for real, yeah. The brain records it all—even background sounds and odors—it's all there. Just have to know how to access it."

He said, "Like computer memory."

"Sort of like that, yeah."

"Could you show me how to do that?"

I said, "Probably. Some day when you have an hour or so free."

He said, "I'm holding you to that. Do you really get five hundred a day?"

I told him, "Well, that's negotiable. More often than not I work for good company and interesting experiences."

"Do I qualify for that rate?"

I said, "So far, sure. Just don't go weird on me."

He chuckled, said, "Look who's talking."

That office was becoming intensely busy, with the homicide technicians doing their thing and the medical examiner preparing to transport the body. They were having a hell of a time because that body was frozen into the seated position. I asked Alvarez to walk me to my car, where I showed him the file from Sloane's office. He flipped through it interestedly, remarked, "I'd like to have a copy of this." So we went back inside and found a coin-operated copier.

As we were parting, the cop told me, "Want you to know that I appreciate your cooperation. I'd like to think that it will continue."

I assured him that I would keep him informed of all developments in my investigation.

He said, "Thanks," and then, following a brief and almost embarrassed pause asked, "Is Miss Amalie an angel?"

I told him, "I'm still working on that."

He said, "Yeah, it's nasty work but someone has to do it, right?"

It was meant as a joke but was right on nevertheless.

Someone, for damn sure, had to do it. It seemed as

though I had been elected. And this day's work could become very nasty indeed.

I wanted to find Windmere Hill and have a little visit with Thomas Sloane, Jim's disabled father. I was thinking that it would be interesting to discover how the elder Sloane regarded his relationship with the mysterious Valentinius.

At that moment I had no inkling—let me assure you—of what I would encounter at Windmere Hill.

I would have gone anyway, of course.

Someone had to do it.

EIGHTEEN

On Windmere Hill

Windmere Hill is a convalescent home for millionaires. It boasts a full medical staff, including a psychiatrist, two geriatric specialists, and a fully accredited gerontologist. Gerontology, I learned, has to do with the scientific study of the aging process, also with the problems of the aged, whereas geriatrics is that branch of medicine that deals with the diseases of old age.

The gerontologist was a fascinating guy, a Dr. Cross— mid-forties, bright-eyed and energetic, sharp of wit and seemingly enamored of challenging conversation.

I drew him by default, all the other professionals being busy with their patients and the administrator insisting that I speak with one of the staff before being allowed to visit Thomas Sloane. He seemed delighted, offering me in turn coffee and chocolate and tea and finally—in hospitable desperation maybe—a snort of bourbon. We sat on a wide veranda at the side of the main building in a beautiful environment of flowering bougainvillea and roses, and I could tell by the way we settled in that this guy wanted to talk, so I was resolved to make it worthwhile.

"What exactly does a gerontologist do?" I asked him, leaving Sloane aside for the moment.

"Around here, not much," he replied with a relaxed laugh. "Afraid I'm here for window dressing. But the pay is excellent and I can virtually write my own research program. I'm available for consultation, of course, and I am a medical doctor so I can help out in emergencies."

"I didn't ask it right," I told him. "Actually I guess I was looking for the difference between geriatrics and gerontology."

Cross scratched his head and replied, "About the same magnitude as, say, a research chemist and a pharmacist. A geriatric doctor treats disease and discomfort in the aged. A gerontologist wonders why disease and discomfort accompany old age."

I asked, "How would you qualify old age?"

He replied, "We have only two directions in life, Ford: up and down. Like firing a gun into the air. The bullet goes up as far as the inherent energy can take it, then it reverses direction and falls to the ground. Life is like that. The explosion of conception sends us hurtling upward. When the inherent energy is spent, we begin collapsing back toward the nothingness we started from. What was the question?"

"How old is old age?"

"Semelparous or iteroparous?"

"What?"

"Depends on the reproductive mode. Semelparous organisms reproduce once and promptly die—not from disease but because they're programmed for it. The process is called senescence or growing old, and for the semelparous it is a very rapid senescence—and definitely programmed. Couldn't say they're old, could you, at the moment of sexual maturity, but the mating triggers senescence, as though their own purpose in life is to reproduce. Once they've done that, what is there to hang around for?"

I said, "Interesting."

"Sure it is. Salmon and eels are semelparous, all of your annual and biannual plants, many insects, but only a very few vertebrates like you and me. No no—" The doctor laughed explosively. "Many married men may feel semelparous, but I assure you that the human species is certifiably iteroparous—most of us screw around as much as we can—however . . . we're talking old age—semelparous forms of life require full vigor right up to the very end so that they may reproduce. So old age for a moth—that is to say, senescence—is a very brief affair, greatly accelerated compared to an ape say—but the moth is not complaining because he enjoyed vigorous life all the way through his entire reproductive life span. The ape will live through maybe fifty percent of his. Old age for this guy began at about midlife."

I said, "Yes, that's fascinating. But how old is old for the human being?"

"In a practical sense," Cross replied, "human senescence begins at about forty—but our clock has been winding down from the moment we reached full maturity. Top of the trajectory, see, and the bullet begins to fall. But what we commonly think of as old age depends a lot on the individual. In gerontology ninety years is given as the life span of man. I would say the last one-third of that is old age. But again, depending on the individual."

"What would you say," I asked him, "if I told you that yesterday I dined with a three-hundred-year-old man who played the piano like Liberace and spoke knowledgeably and interestingly on virtually every subject in the arts and sciences of mankind?"

Those knowing eyes danced with good humor as the doctor replied, "I'd say sell me a ticket to that act. There are outward exceptions to the life span—notably in sections of the USSR, where they claim to have people living for twenty-five to thirty years beyond the century mark, but I'd have to say that a three-hundred-year-old man is an impossibility. We simply don't have the program for it. Aging is a greatly misunderstood process in the common mind. We don't simply grow older. We begin to break up and dissolve. Lean body mass decreases steadily after physical maturity, and dramatically so under senescence— so that a man of ninety will have depleted two-thirds of his mature lean body mass. Basal metabolism decreases as lean mass decreases, everything slows down, the DNA/RNA sequence becomes confused, the immune systems fall apart, the brain loses mass, cells are dying faster than they can be replaced, and even those that survive become less functional, less responsive. So your three-hundred-year-old man must be a bat."

I said, "Whoa! Ever hear of Dracula?"

Cross laughed, said, "Sure, but they got the story all

wrong. It isn't vampirism that gives the bat long life; actually the vampire is one of the shortest-lived bats. The little brown bat—*myotis lucifugus*—has a life span of twenty-four years. That's a hell of a long time for so small a mammal. Has to do with conservation of inherent energy. I'm talking metabolism. The total lifetime energy-burn for man is set at about 1,200,000 calories per gram of tissue. Compare that to 400,000 per gram for your dog or cat. But see, that's tied to brain weight. The highly cephalized animals have a prodigious output of energy, and that feature is tied to longer life span. But a bat is a very small animal with a tiny brain. No way could he live long enough to produce that kind of energy. Yet some of them have very long lives, if you want to call that living. They do it by turning down and conserving energy instead of expending it. Eighty percent of an insectivorous bat's twenty-plus years of life is spent in deep torpor. A house mouse gets about three years—but, oh, he's a bundle of energy while he's here."

I said, "So Dracula . . ."

"Yes, if I had written the story I would have forgotten about the blood sucking and developed a way to reduce the metabolic rate by about twenty-fold through torpid states. Crawl into the coffin, yes, and snooze for several years or several centuries with the metabolism near zero, then come out when the coming was good and party like hell for a couple of nights."

I said, "You lose a lot of friends that way."

He laughed and replied, "And wake up each time to a totally new world. Think I prefer it the way I have it."

I said, "Other than becoming a hibernating animal, do

you see anything in the cards right now for someday greatly extending the human life span?"

"Oh sure, it will come. That's our next big breakthrough. Lot of brilliant people working the problem. Sooner or later someone will find a way to rewrite the genetic program."

I said, "You think it's basically a matter of programming then, despite all that stuff about energy and metabolism."

"Basically, yes," he agreed, "I think so."

We then put Thomas Sloane on the agenda. Cross gave me a bit of patient history and we talked a bit about the quality of care at Windmere Hill. Sloane was under the care of a cardiovascular specialist, a neurologist, and a psychiatrist. He had suffered a massive stroke, sustained severe neurological damage, and appeared to be in a mental state resembling catalepsy. He had been at Windmere Hill for eleven months; he was seventy-five years of age.

Each patient at Windmere Hill enjoyed private quarters and around-the-clock nursing. Even while the patient was asleep, a nurse sat beside the bed. The care was, in Cross's word, immaculate.

"Not that Tom would know it," Cross added with a sad smile. "I'm going to be perfectly frank about this, Ford. As nice as it is, this place is no more than a charnel house. These poor people require constant care and they always will. There is only one way out of here."

I said, "But they hang on. Must be a reason, wouldn't you think?"

He replied, "Sure, because they are being urged to do so, and I think maybe they just don't know how to die. I don't call this living, my friend, what they experience here."

I had to agree with the good doctor when I saw old Tom Sloane. No way could he have weighed a hundred pounds, though in his prime he must have tipped two-hundred easily. He was dressed, but the clothing was falling off him everywhere. And he was seated in a comfortable leather chair facing the window, but he could not have known if it was raining or shining out there.

The thing that really curled me—I mean really knocked me out—was the face of old Tom Sloane. It was not a face but a leathery grimace, thin flesh pulled tautly across that skull and the eyes bugging as though viewing something unspeakably terrible, mouth open in a silent scream.

I muttered, "Good God," and stepped quickly back to speak to Dr. Cross. "How long has he been like that?" I asked.

"Since they brought him here eleven months ago," he replied solemnly. "Responds to nothing."

I had seen that face before, twice, and recently. It had been worn by the younger Sloane as he lay crumpled on the beach below Pointe House. And it had been worn by the boy entrepreneur, Hank Gibson, as the medical examiners fought his stiffened corpse from an office chair.

"Prognosis?" I muttered to Cross.

"Oh, he's terminal. Came in here terminal. Like I said, there's but one way out of here. A mere question of time. For the lucky ones it's a brief senescent climax."

I went around and took the old man's bony hand, forced myself to gaze into those horrified eyes—and then my sense of humanity stirred itself and went inside of him.

It was much worse, in there.

It was chaos, in there.

I moved my other hand to the top of his skull, and I said to him, through the mind, *"Go home, Tom."*

I became aware of a faint clearing from somewhere within the chaos, then I thought I saw movement in the eyes. So I sent it again: *"Go home, Tom. It's all done here. Thank you. Now go home."*

Old Tom Sloane died in my arms.

Thank God, and thank God. I feel sure that that liberated soul sang a happy song all the way to wherever. And mine sang with him.

NINETEEN

Logia

There are those moments in direct experience when you can touch something with the mind and be forever changed in your own perception of who you are and what the human experience is all about. That moment on Windmere Hill was one such revelation for me. I do not pretend to fully comprehend the event, nor could I have said with any certainty at the moment that I understood more about the mystery of Pointe House than at any moment earlier—but I did know that some fresh perspective on the situation was beginning a movement at some level of my own consciousness.

Certainly I had been deeply and strongly moved over the plight of Tom Sloane—though a total stranger—and I felt nothing short of elation over my role in helping him to escape it—but this is not to say that I intellectually understood that plight, the reason behind it, or my almost instinctive response to it.

If you were walking in your neighborhood one evening at dusk and saw a trash can upended and heard a commotion beneath it, stopped to investigate, raised the can, and a small furry animal shot out between your feet and raced away into the gloom before you could get a good look at it—you might draw reasonable conclusions as to the situation and your role in it. But if pressed with questions as to what kind of animal?—how had he gotten there?—why could he not get out on his own?—where did he go when you set him free?—See, the answers to those questions lie outside your direct experience in the matter, so you can respond with surmise only: it might have been a squirrel or a cat; probably searching for food; accidentally turned the can over and became trapped beneath it; too small or confused or panic-stricken to free himself; probably ran straight home, wherever that was, as fast as he could.

That is where I was, see, in my own understanding of Tom Sloane and his plight, but with one important additional factor: I knew that what I had done was right and good, though some may recoil at my intervention in that situation, because I was given the understanding at the moment *that I had discharged an important obligation*, and that the obligation was part and parcel to the mission, whatever that was, in which I was presently engaged.

All of which is a lengthy way of saying that Tom Sloane is no mere footnote to this story; he too *is* the story as much as any other character, and somewhere I knew that, as I came down off Windmere Hill. I just did not understand all that I knew, and I was determined all the more to do so.

But I am going to give you another leg up on me at this point in the story, because I want you to follow it better than I was while I was experiencing it. That means that I have to talk a bit about metaphysics, particularly that branch originating in Neoplatonism—and more particularly, the distinctions elaborated by Plotinus (A.D. 205–270).

As you probably already know, metaphysics is an attempt to elaborate mystery—the ultimate mystery: who and where am I?—who and where is God?—what is the significance of existence?—or, what is it all about? For some it is a meaningless exercise that only confounds the thinking mind and clouds reason and experience. Those people will usually turn to science, economics, history, humanistic philosophy, and/or simple religious faith as a better alternative to frame their existence and sensing of self. Others—more and more others in this modern age—cannot find a satisfactory framework for their own existence in the purely earthbound dimensions of experience, so go seeking the great mystery itself: the basis of all experience; the great Truth behind it all; the origin, the meaning, and the relationships of existence itself. Call it metaphysics— and you may include in there all the parlor games and light diversions that frequently take the name—just do not limit the field by dismissing metaphysics as astrology or spiritualism or sorcery, etc.

Metaphysics is indeed the mother of all religion, all philosophy, all science, all organized pursuits of the human mind. A religion is a *metaphysical system* as is any particular philosophy and science, since metaphysics *provides the framework* through which we approach understanding. The major distinction between a metaphysical system and metaphysics itself is that the *system* has ceased the exploration of reality itself—has come to terms with some concept of what reality is—and now seeks to frame experience within that system.

Neoplatonism is such a system. It is an evolutionary form of various movements all inspired by the *Dialogues* of Plato (428–347 B.C.), and it is important to modern man if for no other reason than that this framework of reality has largely shaped Western man's approach to logical thought. It is difficult to generalize Neoplatonism since there are so many diverging branches, but all of these do embrace a certain consensus of thought built up of these basic elements: a) there are many spheres of being, arranged in a hierarchy of descending order, the last and lowest of these comprising the space–time universe of human sense perception; b) each separate sphere is a product of its next superior sphere, deriving its existence through some process outside of time and space; c) each "derived" being (you and me, angels, spirits, eels and microbes) becomes established in its own reality by reflecting back through contemplative desire toward its superior, such reflection being implicit (or inherent) in the original, outgoing creative impulse received from its superior, so that the entire production may be characterized as a double movement of outgoing and return (action/reaction); d) each sphere is a grosser image or expression of the sphere above it; e) degrees of being (individual spheres) are also degrees of unity; that is, the higher the sphere of being, the greater the degree of unity; conversely, the lower the sphere, the greater the multiplicity or separateness of individual beings. The ramifications here, at the lowest possible level, are toward the subatomic individualization of matter in space–time; whereas, f) the supreme sphere, and through it all of existence in any sense, is derived from the ultimate principle itself (science's First Cause or "singularity"), which utterly transcends any conceptualized or conceivable reality to the point that the ultimate principle is said to be "beyond being," without limitation of any kind. Since it has no limitation and cannot be subdivided by attributes or qualifications of any nature, it also really cannot be named but should be called "the One" as an indication of its total simplicity.

Got that? Total simplicity. We descend into the chaos of total individuation and infinite complexity, ascend toward and into the ultimate simplicity where all is one and one is all.

This utter simplicity is the source of all perfections as well as the ultimate goal of return from chaos. The out-and-back double movement constituting the hierarchy of derived reality emanates from the One and returns to the One.

Got it? If the supreme simplicity cannot be determined by reference to any specific traits or attributes, then man's knowledge of it cannot be anything like any other kind of knowledge, since it is not an object (a thing) and nothing known to man can be applied to it; therefore the One can be known only if and when, *by its own direct action*, it embraces the mind of man in some mystical union with itself, an event which cannot be imagined or described.

Much of Christian theology is derived from this Neoplatonic model of existence. Plotinus himself was not a Christian, but he was taught by Ammonius, who also taught the Christian Origen who became one of the most respected and influential of all early Christian thinkers.

Plotinus saw the goodness and beauty of the material universe as the best possible work of Soul, but man was also a work of Soul—and, as Soul, man in his essence could never be limited or harmed by worldly imperfection because, as souls within bodies, men can exist on any level of the soul's experience and activity.

Did you catch that *souls within bodies*? Souls always have bodies, whatever the sphere or plane, but each ascending sphere requires and provides an appropriately finer body of expression.

We can also move back and forth along the ladder, falling and rising among the various spheres of being, ascending in spirit to the level of Universal Soul or falling with a crash into the gross vicissitudes of space–time experience encased in flesh.

Plotinus also believed that the soul could travel from the fleshy sphere to commune in the higher spheres without disturbing or interrupting the earthly duties of that soul.

Which brings us, I guess, back to our story.

Who or what was Valentinius de Medici, and what the hell was going on here? Was he fallen angel or pilgrim soul, black magician or enlightened mystic, demonic manifestation or time traveler, con man or confused ghost?

And what was the secret of Pointe House? Who were those people there? What were they trying or hoping to achieve, or were they just hanging out for lack of anything better to do with their time? Or was time relative to whatever it was they were up to?

Was Pointe House a way station between spheres, a warp in space, a wrinkle in time—or was it just a sentimental anachronism like the town itself, fighting for the truth about itself?

What was this weird arrangement with the Sloanes, and how or why had it engulfed them? Why was Gibson involved to the point of extinction, and what was behind the mask of horror that seized them all?

And why, God tell me why, was a beautiful young artist with a master's touch caught up in all this, to the point of a possible split personality and an apparent morbid compulsion to paint an array of ghosts with a common soul. And who after all did she intend to show it to, on a deadline that coincided with that other crisis—or were both the same?

My life is never simple—and I do love a mystery—but I had the definite feeling that the thing was out of hand this time.

I frankly did not know where the hell to go next.

So you go figure it for me, please. Haul out your own metaphysical system as a guide, or use the one I outlined above, and try to make some sense of it.

Just remember that the routine to simplicity is an ascending one and that you and I in present form occupy the sphere of chaos.

So have a go at it, please, and lend me a hand with this mess.

Meanwhile I'm on my way to have another go at the beautiful young painter/sculptress.

Want to know why she does not know what she ought to know. Also want to know why she does what she's doing, and who she's painting/sculpting for.

Ready? Let's go.

TWENTY

Mission Control

I hit the Laguna cliffs again at midafternoon and tried to get a fix on the spot outside the estate where Jim Sloane's abandoned car had been found by the police. Pointe House is situated outside the city limits in a county area. The parking on Pacific Coast Highway is very spotty along that stretch, just a broad shoulder here and there. The entry onto the point occupied one of those broad areas extending a hundred feet or so to either side of the drive, all of which was posted against parking. I took mental note of all that and went on through to the point without pause.

Francesca was in her studio, very expertly applying framing to a large seascape. She looked up with a troubled frown as I entered but quickly returned her attention to the job at hand without greeting me or otherwise acknowledging my presence. So I browsed around for a minute or two, toured the studio looking for the stuff I'd seen in there the night before. It was not there; none of it was there.

So I went to the framing table and asked the petulant lady, "Already crated up your show?"

She replied, "Ha ha, very funny. Not sure I'm going to *have* a show, at this rate. Please get out of here and leave me alone."

So I took a leap, and told her: "Francesca . . . you had a show last night. Right here. There were more than forty paintings, and an equal number of sculptures. It was devastating stuff—I'm talking master works, absolutely stunning portraits such as I have never seen before by any painter."

She put down her tools, folded her arms across her chest, fixed me with a penetrating gaze and asked in a tight little voice, "What are you trying to do to me? You wander in here off the street and just take over the place, follow me around like a puppy dog and stand in my face while I'm trying to work; then you tell outrageous lies to the police and make me look like some kind of jerk—now you're telling me . . ."

I had to know the truth, so I told her, "You forgot to mention that I also made love to you on the beach."

We had a stare-down over that one. Lasted for, I guess, twenty seconds or so. She had to have seen the truth in my eyes. Finally she dropped the defiant gaze and dropped her shoulders and said very softly, "Damn it."

I asked, "Is it becoming more and more common, these lapses of memory?"

The voice was dulled as she replied, "I don't know what you're talking about."

"Sure you do. You suffer memory gaps. You find yourself here, and don't know how you got here; there, and don't recall going there or why. You don't remember screwing my brains out on the beach yesterday afternoon, don't remember dinner and partying last night, don't remember showing me your portrait gallery at midnight, don't remember—"

"Okay, okay, stop it!"

I said, "Something of a nightmare, isn't it."

That broke her. She turned away from me with tears in the eyes and marched to the window; stood there arms folded and staring broodingly out to sea. I went over and hugged her from behind, held onto her, told her, "That's why I'm here, Francesca. Valentinius asked me to come and help you. I want to do that. But you—"

"How could he know?" she asked in the small voice. "I've seen him only twice, and that was . . . some time ago."

I said, "Yes, but he sees you. Every day."

She shivered in my light embrace, turned her face into my shoulder, whispered, "Who is he?"

I whispered back, "I think he may be your guardian angel."

That lovely head dropped and the shoulders began to quiver. I thought at first that she was crying. But she was laughing. Laughing.

I said, "Is that so funny?"

Francesca extricated herself from my grasp and turned about to look at me as she replied, "I thought I was the crazy one. But—sorry, I have to say this—if one of us is crazy, it is not me, Mr. Ford."

I reminded her, "But a man is dead, you see. In fact,

Miss Amalie, since I arrived here yesterday, three men closely connected to this house have died. If you cannot get your act together enough to offer a coherent account of yourself to the police, then you may be in very real trouble."

She gave me a sober inspection then smiled and replied, "Then let my guardian angel handle it."

I told her, "I'm his proxy." I hauled out the power of attorney, gave it to her.

She quickly scanned it and gave it back, said in a vague voice, "I didn't know angels needed proxies."

"Me neither, but maybe sometimes they do. Look, I don't know who Valentinius is. But I do believe that you could be in more danger already than any cop could throw at you. And I do sincerely believe that is why I am here."

I gave her a brief sketch of my "professional" background, then related my encounter with Valentinius at Malibu. She let me talk, offering no comments and requesting no elaboration beyond what I gave her. When I had given her all that I intended to give, she asked me, "So what kind of danger do you think I'm in?"

So I let her have it, directly and bluntly: "Cohabitation danger, possibly. Or, beyond that, total takeover. You are presently providing bodily expression for two distinct personalities. Both have artistic talent—one just beginning to realize herself, the other no less than a master. I have seen the work of both. The master had her show last night. It was a wow. Better than what I see here today, but that difference is very subtle; the master is present also in the student, and that presence is unmistakable. But you may be moving toward total assimilation. That worries me, and I think we need to work on it."

The lady was plainly frightened. "What does that mean: total assimilation?"

I explained, "Permanent loss of the student."

"You mean . . . ?"

"Uh huh. She's taking you over, kid."

It was not a total buy. Francesca was scared, yes—wouldn't you be?—but after all I am not certified for medical diagnoses and the lady hardly knew me. I can be persuasive though when I need to be—so at least I had her attention to the extent that she was not willing to simply shrug the whole thing off and walk away. She admitted to the lapses of memory and told me that indeed they seemed to be occurring more and more frequently.

She also talked of her background—born and raised in California, Austrian ancestry, studied at CalArts but left without graduating—couldn't bend herself to the will of her instructors—worked briefly at a day-care center, then as a cocktail waitress while studying days under a private art teacher, gravitated to Laguna along the art trail.

She had talked a local restaurateur into hanging several of her paintings on his walls, and one day a man came to see her about commissioning a portrait. The man was Valentinius. One thing led to another—weird things—and she found herself "transported bag and baggage" to Pointe House. She had not seen her benefactor since.

Instead of being fired up over this apparent leap of fortune, Francesca had at first found it difficult to concentrate on her work at Pointe House. She'd taken to long sojourns on the beach, idle daydreaming, killing time. Then she became interested in yoga, shortly thereafter discovering a video tape on postures and breathing exercises, and Hai Tsu began instructing her in various Taoist disciplines.

The daydreaming evolved into meditation techniques and yogic purifications. There were periods of confusion with out of body experiences and dreamlike trance states. And she began to disremember, a purification technique that came to her in a dream, through which she encouraged replacement of real memories by "dream-stuff."

But Francesca had not thought of herself as being in trouble. She realized that she had become different but she greeted the change as growth and self-realization. The memory lapses were only vaguely troubling; she dismissed them as preoccupation, which was easy to do once she again became fired up over her work and was spending long hours in the studio.

Four weeks before my arrival at Pointe House, Valentinius contacted her by telephone and told her that he'd arranged an "important" exhibition of her work, that she had six weeks to prepare for it. She did not at that time have a single work that she considered worthy of exhibition, so she threw herself into the challenge with renewed vigor—often working eighteen to twenty hours a day in her studio—usually so lost in the work that day blended unnoticeably into night and, frequently, consciousness into unconsciousness in baffling patterns that found her waking up while walking across the room or strolling along the beach.

It was a classic pattern, in my freaky world.

And the more Francesca talked, the more convinced I became that she was definitely in trouble.

I guess she could read my reactions because also the more she talked the more troubled she became.

We ended up by taking the elevator to the beach where she could "let the salt air cool my brain" while we walked and talked. She showed me a wind cave in the rocks, accessible only at low tide, through which we intended to gain access to the open far side of the point, but we did not get that far.

That wind cave provided access to more than the other side of the promontory. A narrow crevice in there was bringing wind from a third direction; it caught my attention and I paused for a closer inspection; discovered a bend just inside the crevice and an opening large enough to admit a person of my size and agility—faint light just beyond and a sound like wind chimes inviting me to enter.

I looked at Francesca and Francesca looked at me. I asked her, "Shall we?"—and she replied, "Why not?"—so we accepted the invitation.

And found not my dream-state mission control center—but instead perhaps, paradise itself.

It was paradise to me, pal.

I believe it was paradise for Francesca too if I can take her at her word.

We made love again, this time slow and sweet and savorous—and this was definitely Francesca I, the girl next door. We did it on the rocks, surrounded by sparkling tidal pools filled with life and purpose, in a high-domed chamber lit by three converging shafts of light from somewhere high above—and she deliriously told me several times, "Surely I would have remembered this."

For myself, I could never forget it.

But more was involved here than she and me.

Dream state or whatever, I had been inside that chamber before . . . and I believed that she had too. We had been there together, in precisely the same way and with the same overpowering feeling for each other.

But I knew that we would never, ever, be there together again. Don't ask how I knew; I just knew. And I knew too that Francesca Amalie—by whatever name—was the mate that God had made for me.

Paradise, yeah; I'd found it . . . only to lose it perhaps forever—this time around for sure. But I did not know that yet.

TWENTY-ONE

Contemporaries

I guess we both lost awareless of time until natural forces reimpressed it upon our romantic idyll. The cold Pacific was advancing upon us and the light from above was somewhat more muted when Francesca stirred in my arms then sat bolt upright with a concerned cry. The tide had risen and was beginning to fill the chamber with closely successive surges; already the narrow opening was under water even during the recessive ebb of the waves.

"We'll have to swim out!" Francesca gasped.

"Fat chance," I told her. I could hear the surf pounding onto the rock directly outside, and I had seen it earlier from above at high tide. The fury of the attack upon those rocks was an awesome sight; anyone caught in that maelstrom would be reduced to hamburger faster than he could think about it.

I knew that our only chance lay in elevated retreat. We grabbed our clothing and began searching for such a possibility; found one in the form of a narrow ledge projecting from the darkened back wall at about the level of my shoulders. It was uptilted just a bit and looked as though it would provide secure footing if nothing else, so I hoisted Francesca up, threw the clothing onto the ledge, then managed to pull myself up sufficiently to hook the smooth lip with a foot and slide aboard sideways. Picture that as a nude action please—bare skin and all appendages against sheer rock—but it really was not all that bad. I discovered why as soon as I got there. The surface was smooth and slippery. Francesca was not there, and the clothing was not there. Neither was I, for long.

I told you that the ledge appeared to be projecting from the wall at an upward tilt. Actually, it was projecting *through* the wall with about four feet of headroom, almost like a chute providing access to another chamber beyond that wall. As I said, it was slippery. It was also deeply inclined, and I knew a moment of consternation when I realized that I was sliding into a black void. I tried to twist about for a finger hold on the outer lip but I was already beyond that point. I could hear Francesca's frightened pantings directly ahead, but I had already collided with her before I could gather my wits toward any attempt at communications.

She grabbed me and clung for dear life—too scared to even speak I guess—and, yeah, it was scary; she was entitled. We were in utter darkness; God knew where; but there was a bright side, and I tried to make that point: "Least it's dry," I told Francesca.

But it was also very quiet.

I could not hear the surf, or anything else.

For the first time in my life in fact I understood what it meant to be as quiet as the grave. Our breathing and our heartbeats were all the ear could hear.

Francesca must have been entertaining similar thoughts. She whispered to me, "Are we...what are...are we dead?"

I chuckled as I replied, "If so, we came down on the bad side. Always heard the path to hell was greased and slippery."

"Very funny," she said, but she was not laughing with me.

I found our clothing and tried the cigarette lighter. It was dry and functional, its flame bright and straight in the still environment, and it revealed to us the immediate dimensions of our "grave." We were in a narrow cavern, about a yard wide at the floor, with sloping walls that converged to form the uneven ceiling at varying levels— hardly more than a crawl space at the tighter points but it appeared to twist along in a more or less horizontal fashion and to extend beyond the reach of our light.

There was not enough light to reach to the top of the chute that had deposited us there, and I could not hazard a guess as to its length, but I knew without more than tentatively trying that it was going to be a hell of a difficult climb out of there. So I suggested that we venture on and see what lay at the other end of our crawl space.

I was thinking of my dream you see—the mission control dream—and wondering if it had been precognitive in some way, as many dreams are, especially many of my dreams. And since it would be many hours yet before the tide began to ebb, even an exit via the chute was not a practical option at the moment.

I offered to venture on alone but Francesca would not hear of it. We struggled into our clothing and I made a leash of my belt, forming a loop with the buckle at my ankle. Francesca twisted the other end around her hand and we set off single file on hands and knees. It was slow going along the uneven rocky surface and a bit rough on the knees, but I got no complaints from Francesca and we moved steadily forward through many twists and turns for probably ten minutes—pausing now and then to hit the lighter and check our surroundings—before I saw the faint glow at the end of the tunnel.

"Light ahead," I announced with a happy grunt.

Francesca panted, "Thank you, God."

"Don't thank him yet," I cautioned. "Could be no more than a tiny vent like those above the tidal chamber."

She said, "Has to be more than that. I could not possibly go back."

We lay there and rested for a couple of minutes and talked to cheer each other. I said, "Sorry, kid; really didn't have all this in mind when we left the house."

She said, "Who even had a mind when we left the house? But you're not really sorry for what happened, are you? I'm not."

I replied, "Sorry for that, no; for this, yes. Feel like a jerk. Should've known better. *Did* know better. Just lost the time."

She said, "Hey, it's my beach. I damn well knew better. And I feel like the chicken who went back for his feather."

"What chicken was that?" I asked.

"You know, the joke about the chicken who lost a tail feather while crossing the road. Went back to get it and a car ran over his head. Lost his head over a little piece of tail. That's me."

I said, "Well gee, thanks. Just a little piece of tail, eh? That's all it was?"

She giggled tiredly, replied, "Okay, so it was a big piece. We still lost our heads, didn't we?"

I said, "Well it's not hardly worth it if you don't, is it. Speaking strictly for myself, Ma'am, it was worth it."

She said, "Thanks. Isn't that what I said?"

"You said a lot of things," I reminded her. "But I'll chalk it up to the heat of the moment, if you'd like."

"*What* did I say?"

"Said you love me. Always have, always will. Said we've walked the star trails together."

She laughed lightly, a bit self-consciously. "Must have been the other me."

I said, "Okay."

She said quickly, "No, it was me. Really me. I remember every lovely moment of it. And I remember some things that you said too."

I said, "Okay."

"You said God had me in mind when he created woman."

"Okay."

"And he had you in mind when he created me."

"I said that?"

"You sure did."

I said, "Must've been the other me."

She jerked on my leash and said, "Rat."

We went on then and a couple of minutes later emerged into a large chamber much like the tidal cave but much larger.

It looked, yeah, like the mission control center in my dream—very much like it except without the equipment. There were tiered levels though, and I could not see to the end of it. Like the tidal cave it all lay beneath a tremendous domed ceiling and was lit naturally from high above. The air in there was good and dry and even sweetly scented.

And, well, there was *some* equipment in there, if you want to call it that. Several long tables—looked like stainless steel—occupied a slightly raised level along one wall. They were clean, spotless even, and not a thing upon them. And set into the rock wall behind the tables were a number of vaultlike doors made out of the same stuff; I call them doors for want of a better name: think of a circular wall safe with a door about twenty-four inches in diameter but just set flush into the wall with no handle or keyway or anything else to make it open.

Or—maybe this is better as a simile—think of the cold-storage section of a modern morgue, where the bodies are kept in sliding drawers behind little round doors.

Francesca seemed a bit dazed by the whole thing. She stood exactly in the same spot where she'd emerged from the tunnel, hands on hips and gawking at the natural wonder. I had to call her name twice to get her attention and show her the man-made wonder.

"What do you suppose it is?" she asked in a hushed voice.

"Well I don't think it's a kitchen," I replied. "What do you think?"

She said, "It's warm in here. Why do you think it's so warm?"

I said, "Some sort of natural heating probably. Have you ever heard of hot springs in this area?"

She shook her head, ran a finger along a shiny table, looked at the finger, remarked, "No dust. Why is there no dust? How did they get this stuff in here? Surely not the way we came."

I asked, "They *who*?"

She said, "They whoever put this here. When, do you think?"

I said, "Hell, I don't know." I was probing with a fingernail around a steel cylinder or whatever in the wall; could not find a crack or chink anywhere. I told Francesca, "It's like the rock wall cooled from a molten state around this thing."

She said, "That's ridiculous. Isn't it? This rock must have formed millions and millions of years ago. They didn't have stainless steel back then. Did they?"

I said, "Not unless there's a lot we don't know about dinosaurs."

I took my lady by the hand then and led her out of there.

I knew the way, you see.

I'd been there before.

Whether in a dream or as a contemporary of the dinosaurs, I could not have said.

But I knew the way.

We ascended natural stairs that had been cut into the rock by some means affording laserlike precision, and came onto a large shelf near the dome of the chamber. As we turned and looked down, I saw the fire in Francesca's eyes and knew that she too was getting a flicker from another time.

She gasped, "Oh God, Ash. It looks so familiar."

Familiar, yeah, that's how it looked.

And I was beginning to get a feeling about the secret of Pointe House and a two-hundred-year-old land grant that had to be protected at all costs.

Just a feeling, sure . . . but a very familiar feeling, and maybe even contemporary—who knows?—with the dinosaurs.

TWENTY-TWO

Bodies Terrestrial

We emerged via a pivoting rock door into the pit of the elevator shaft. The cage was still there, resting on the bottom stop just above our heads. Circular steps in the rock took us easily around the machinery in the pit and deposited us on the rock ledge in front of the cage. I had noted those steps earlier and assumed them to be for maintenance access to the elevator machinery.

Francesca seemed a bit dazed. Maybe I was too. She was watching the surf, now well above the little wind cave, as it crashed onto the rocky point and I knew what she was thinking. I too was doing a bit of projection into that hillside and trying to relate the location of the tidal chamber from this point of view. It could have been a watery death for us in there—that much was obvious; it was a sobering view.

She stood beside me with an arm encircling my waist and told me, "I have felt a fascination for this beach from the first time I saw it. I even come down sometimes in the middle of the night and stand right where we're standing now and watch the surf climb the rocks."

I said, "Yes, it's beautiful."

"More than that," she said. "It's more than that."

"In what way, do you think?"

She shrugged, shivered, clasped me more tightly, said, "It's cold out here, isn't it."

Compared to inside the mountain, yes; there was quite a difference in temperature. But I wanted to pursue the more-than-that idea. I said, "You told me yesterday, Francesca—the other you told me—when we were together on the sand that you first came here from Vienna in the year 1872."

"I told you that?"

"The other you told me that."

"Then the other me must be crazy as a loon, wouldn't you say?"

I said, "Maybe not. The real you told me earlier today that your ancestry is Austrian."

"Are you suggesting that the other me is actually my . . . what?—grandmother?—great-grandmother? Let's see, 1872 would be . . ."

"Roughly five generations back."

"Then that would make her . . ."

"Three greats back, more or less."

Francesca gave me a murky look. "How did she get here?"

I gave her one back. "Valentinius brought her."

"Valen . . . the same . . . *our* Valentinius?"

I said, "It seems there's only been one."

Francesca shivered again and said, "I want to go up now."

So we stepped into the elevator cage and returned to the house. She'd gone silent on me, wrapped in dark thought and withdrawn throughout the ascent. When we emerged into the atrium I knew that the other Francesca was back. She was cool to me, almost rude—well okay, downright rude and more hostile than cool.

"You were brought here to mind the store," she said haughtily as we crossed the entryway, "not to sample the merchandise."

I replied, "Is that what this is?—a store? And the merchandise is bodies terrestrial? Or is it bodies celestial?"

"Don't be impertinent, Ashton. You know very well what I meant."

I said, "I think you're jealous."

"Damned right I'm jealous," she replied.

She left me standing there scratching my head and strode off toward the studio. Hell, I let her go. It had been a long day already. I wanted a shower, a bit of rest, some time alone to think.

I guess I knew instinctively that it was going to be an even longer night.

It certainly was.

See, we have a mix-and-match mystery going here. Bodies terrestrial or bodies celestial? Or maybe both? How 'bout neither? Bodies celestial have no need of subterranean chambers or mechanical contrivances. Technology is the artifice of bodies terrestrial, but what manner of those could have developed life-prolonging techniques hundreds of years ago when the cutting edge of modern medical technology is still frustrated in that quest?

Take a guy like St. Germain now. Was he really a de Medici and heir to the throne of Transylvania?—or was that just a convenient cover of mystery for a body celestial with a terrestrial mission? If the former, then why did the man stalk the royal halls of Europe throughout that century of prologue to the modern age instead of claiming his own inheritance and becoming a historical figure in his own right? Why would he range far and wide in secret and hazardous missions for the throne of France, dabble in technology and alchemy and metaphysics, set up laboratories and manufactures and turn them over to others—and never have a real life or identity of his own? As a real person—a terrestrial—Le Comte de St. Germain makes no sense at all, not even if he did find a way to greatly extend his own life span.

If, on the other hand, St. Germain was really a celestial, at least the mystery itself makes sense. And who is to say how much influence, within that mystery, his being here had on the course of human history. History as narrative is necessarily greatly abridged and is made up of final impressions, not active details. Historians are not seers; they are merely impressionists and convey to us their impression of the relativity of events.

But if St. Germain is celestial—and if St. Germain is also Valentinius and therefore Valentinius is celestial— then why all this involvement with things terrestrial? Why Pointe House and legal problems and hollowed-out mountains beside the sea? Why, indeed, the two talents and two personalities of Francesca Amalie? And why the hell is Ashton Ford mixed into it?

Why so much death in an atmosphere of immortality, and why all the weird characters-in-residence in a mansion fit for royalty?

For royalty?

Uh *huh*.

Call Pointe House a castle then, and remember that all self-respecting castles have dungeons. Recast your mystery into terms of things celestial and things terrestrial and try to keep the two separated until both strands come together at the true moment of crisis.

Do that, and you'll have another leg up on me as I retire to the royal suite to rest and repair all my bodies while I try to figure out some way to exercise my proxy.

Or was I doing that already?

I got my shower okay, but the rest of it was not in the cards—not, that is, with Hai Tsu in the picture. She is a very dutifully determined young woman, and I had a hell of a time keeping her out of my bathroom. Also a locked door seems to mean nothing whatever to her. Whether by passkey or whatever, she comes and goes as she damn well pleases. I don't know; maybe walls mean nothing to her either. I do know that I showed her to the door twice—the last time rather forcefully—but still she was standing there holding a big terry cloth towel for me when I stepped out of the shower.

I was feeling very exasperated but also probably a bit

resigned to it as I told her, "Damn it, Hai Tsu, this really isn't necessary. I can dry my own damned back."

She said, "Yes, Shen," and went right on drying it for me.

So hell, I lit a cigarette and stalked around naked while she laid out clothes for the evening. I figured, what the hell, let's get some mileage out of this, so I asked her, "Who's for dinner tonight?"

Those dark eyes glinted joyfully as she replied, "The same, Shen."

I said, "Same old same old, eh? Don't you ever get tired of this?"

"Oh no, Shen. Hai Tsu very happy."

I asked, "How long?"

"How long? Is name?"

I had to laugh. It did sound like a Chinese name. I explained, "No, I meant how long have you been at this?"

"Many year, Shen."

"How many is that?"

"Hai Tsu very privileged. Hai Tsu very happy."

Hai Tsu also cagey as hell.

I asked her, "When did you come here?"

"Come with Shen. Long ago. Hai Tsu come China, long ago. Shen come China, long ago. Hai Tsu very privileged serve Shen. Is Shen not happy with Hai Tsu?"

I said wearily, "Wait a minute. Too many shens make it confusing. You call me Ash. Okay? I am not Shen, I am Ash. Okay?"

"Okay, Ash Shen."

Ashen was what I was by this time. But I thought she'd worked it out rather well.

"When did you come China with Valentinius Shen?"

She never lost the adorational joy but something else was mixing with it now—something maybe just a little nervous or apprehensive. "Hai Tsu must serve Ash Shen, his every wish. Does Ash Shen wish Hai Tsu violate honorable conduct?"

I looked at my hands and told her, "No, Hai Tsu, I don't want you to do that."

She kissed my hand, said, "Dinner in one hour, Ash Shen," and walked toward the door.

I went part of the way with her, asked her, "Have you been in the caves?"

She turned back to look at me from the closed doorway. "Caves, Shen?"

"Under the house. Within the mountain. Have you been there?"

"Ash Shen has been there?" she countered, surprising me with her forwardness.

I said, "Yes. Francesca and I were trapped in the tidal chamber by the rising tide. We found our way out through the caves. I was just wondering if you knew about them."

I saw her then, for the first time, without joy. The lovely face went totally blank as she replied, "Tides very dangerous, Shen. Be very careful. Do not go there again."

I told her, "I have to go again, Hai Tsu. I must pierce the mystery if I am to be of help here."

She was still a total blank as she replied to that. "Caves

come China, Ash Shen, long ago. You must not go there again."

And then—I swear—just like Valentinius, Hai Tsu simply winked out on me. She did not step through that doorway; did not even open the door. She simply flat disappeared.

TWENTY-THREE

Things Celestial

I have been exposed to weirdness for most of my life you know. Still, I do not find it easy or acceptable to simply shrug away weird things when I encounter them. The more, in fact, that I am exposed to this sort of thing, the more insistent becomes the need to understand.

I mean like if you've never had a three-dimensional object wink out right before your eyes, then you've probably never felt any strong need to understand how something like that could happen. But it does happen, and much more frequently than you might imagine. If it happens with you, you are probably either going to convince yourself that it did not happen or else you are likely to go batty trying to understand how it did happen. If it keeps happening, time and again, then you might start to wonder about your sanity.

For myself I had long ago worked out a handy little syllogism to keep myself centered in the confrontations with weirdness. Goes like this: *major premise*, reality is infinite and eternal; *minor*, man is finite and temporal; *therefore*, all of mankind combined within space and time can never experience all that is real.

So what do I know? We can believe anything, but we can know only that which we have experienced. Tell an aborigine who has never been exposed to Newton and celestial mechanics that up is really down and that he moves about and has his being suspended by the feet from the outer surface of a sphere spinning through space, and that aborigine will smile tolerantly and go right on living on his flat earth where obviously his feet are down and his head is up.

The major difference between the aborigine and most of thee and me lies in the fact that most of thee and me have been properly indoctrinated into believing most of anything that we may read, especially the pronouncements of any vague authority, whereas the aborigine has not cultivated the luxury of relying on secondhand information; this guy lives in a very direct relationship with his environment and depends for his survival upon the terms of that relationship. The world to him is real and immediate, never abstract or even potential: it is what he experiences.

But thee and me live in a world that has been defined for us by other minds. In order for us to accept that world, we often must refute the evidence of our senses and we must do so trustingly else all is chaos; therefore the pronouncements that define our world must come from authority and with authority. Never mind that there is no true authority beneath the heavens. Doesn't really matter anyway whether the definition is right or wrong; it matters only that we all accept it as right and that we behave in accordance with that acceptance.

Which is why we get into trouble with weirdness—that which falls outside the orderly definition of reality that binds us together in common mind. Or common *sense*.

So . . . physical objects that can be measured, weighed, and perceived by the senses are said to exist within space and time and therefore must *submit* to the laws laid down by our authorities for the behavior of objects in space and time.

That is why so many of our thinkers have so much trouble with flying saucers and close encounters of any kind. Those saucers and those encounters do not obey the paradigm. In the first place, nothing is allowed to move that way in space–time; second, nothing is allowed to *live* long enough in space–time to bridge the enormous distances within the galaxies. These thinkers should try my little syllogism; perhaps it would help them as it has helped me to leap the mind beyond dogmatism and into the realization that all the scientists and philosophers and preachers combined who have ever lived on this planet have not yet experienced all of reality. They have, in fact, only just begun man's exploration into the mysteries of existence.

So I reserve a small void within my own common sense within which I may examine various items of direct experience that seem to be colored weird. And I try to not freak out when the impossible suddenly seems possible.

That covers just about all things celestial—even flying saucers and all close encounters of the shivery kind.

But we really do not have to go celestial in order to examine the phenomena that were afoot at Pointe House. Actually one needs go no further than the time dilation phenomena of Einstein's general theory of relativity and the specious time of William James—also the view of reality afforded by quantum physics shows that the human world is largely a construct arising from the peculiarity of sense perceptions and synthesized within the brain: that is, from the total recipe of all that is, our brain reacts to only those few ingredients to which it is particularly attuned and cannot even sample the others except in theory.

Thus reality for us is that part of the whole which our brains can discriminate.

To say that anything whatever is impossible is to say that our brains have sampled all of the possibilities of existence and this ain't one of those. It simply ain't true. We are mere infants in this matter of possibility sampling—still 99 percent blind, 99 percent deaf, and 99.8 percent stupid. Ask the newborn babe about the physical act that brought him into this existence; ask him about investments for his college education; ask him what he wants to be when he grows up. You may as well ask him for a description of God. The possible reality to that newborn babe is a warm nipple upon a comforting breast; don't ask him to define existence beyond that experience.

In any realistic analysis the impossible boils down to merely the inexperienced; the impossibility is merely that which is not commonly experienced. So let's not attempt to lay down the law to those who are doing something we cannot do. Let's not call Hai Tsu back into the room and demand that she leave it in a proper way, the way we do to a child who leaves the door ajar. Instead let's try to figure out how Hai Tsu did that—and maybe even wonder if we can do it too.

Apparently St. Germain did it as a common experience. This is one of the ways he "astonished" the courts of Europe. Let's go back a moment and consider the eighteenth-century world of astonishments. It was ruled by a relatively small number of individuals connected by birth and anointed by God himself to rule. Even the church—especially the church—observed and encouraged this hierarchical order of reality; it was the worst tyrant of all and defended its preeminent position through every manner of forceful coercion and atrocity.

But this was not just the eighteenth-century world: it was the real world of mankind *from that point backward* into the total history of man as man.

That order—that old order of things—began toppling during the recorded time of Le Comte de St. Germain. The new world order that arose in its place is the present real world of mankind in the general sense. We still have popes, yes, and petty tyrants and even institutionalized tyrannical governments—but all of us inhabit the new reality in which at least lip service is given to the idea of the essential nobility of every man—human dignity, equality, and rights to self-determination.

It was not that way before St. Germain.

I do not say with any sense of certainty that his influence added one ounce to the weight of the present reality. Indeed the record indicates that St. Germain was a friend of royalty and sympathetic to their eighteenth-century plight with the world rising up against them—but that record is fragmentary at best and totally obliterated in the overall tapestry woven by recognized historians of the era. We do not know precisely whom the mysterious figure operated upon, nor do we know his various strategems, psychologies, modes of operation; we know only that the man was there at virtually every trouble spot and at crucial moments in the unfolding history of the time.

Most of what we get of St. Germain is the record of *astonishment* that accompanied him wherever he went.

I believe that St. Germain was of the order of things celestial. And let us now define things celestial as the full range of all impossibilities of human experience as we commonly identify those today.

In the order of things celestial time is a mere convenience of human perception—which is to say that both past and future are present now; space is that theater into which all of physical existence swirls in patterns only now and then perceptible by our sensory probes; existence itself is a matter of infinite possibility unbounded and unconditioned by *anything* imaginable to the human mind.

Things celestial constitute all of man's impossibilities.

Got that? If so then you are now ready to travel with me into the longest night of my life. Time, you know, is always relative. And it can stand still.

TWENTY-FOUR

Transported

Caves come China, eh? Okay. We'd see about that.

Right now I wanted to know where the money was coming from, so I called a friend in Switzerland who loves to play with computers. He's on the faculty of the Center for Strategic Studies in Berne, an internationally respected scholar; it would damage him to mention his name here, so let's just call him Sam. Sam is the most ingenious computer hacker I have ever come upon. Once, on a dare, he hacked in on a super security Kremlin mainframe, accessing it by telephone through a Russian embassy in the West, and got out of it undetected. Man's a genius. I suspect also that he is a bit of a silicon psychic, but he won't admit to that. I've done a bit of small-time hacking myself, but nowhere in Sam's league.

I gave him the numbers of the Swiss accounts that had

been feeding Sloane, Sloane and James—also several transaction codes for steerage—and he seemed as happy as a kid on Christmas morning to work the problem for me, even though the nine-hour time difference put my voice into his ear in the middle of his night.

It could take a while even for Sam to crack that money mystery but he promised to get right on it. Meanwhile I had all the mystery a mind could handle boiling up all around me. I decided I wanted some real-world objectivity to keep me anchored, so I called Sergeant Alvarez and invited him to dinner. He sounded a bit surprised by the invitation but quickly accepted. Then I called Hai Tsu and told her to set another place for dinner.

She seemed a bit disturbed by that but gave me no argument, responding simply, "Yes, Ash Shen. Name of guest, please?"

I replied, "Alvarez. One of the policemen who were here today. Any problem with that?"

"No, Shen. What does Alvarez Sergeant eat?"

I told her, "Anything that's free, probably. Don't worry about it. He probably won't touch a bite, anyway."

Then I finished dressing and sat down with the Sloane file to study the architectural records of this castle beside the sea. Apparently there had been several major additions and renovations over the years, numerous small ones, but the original foundations had not been altered in any way. The latest major renovation had occurred twenty years earlier and involved also the addition of several sleeping suites on the upper levels, including the one I now occupied, and the conversion of a ballroom into the studio now used by Francesca.

All in all the record was one of almost continuous updating and upgrading, though the original structural dimensions had remained more or less constant.

For what?

Tons of money had been poured into the place, with tons more going for purely custodial care.

For whose benefit?

The building abstracts could not give me that answer, so I went out seeking it for myself. I explored the entire joint from top to bottom and back to top again. What I found was pretty much what I'd seen already, just more of it. Ten suites nearly identical to mine but each one reflecting a different personality, different clothing styles, different cultural tastes—yet no sign of human habitation—that is, no personal stamp, except in Francesca's suite; and she was so clearly evident there, though absent at the moment, as to accentuate the lack of the other suites. Know what I mean? Those other suites were filled with clothing and various personal items but they were like movie sets—stage dressing. I got no feeling of *people* there.

I even invaded the domestics' quarters. They were all busy in the kitchen so I let myself into the small apartment and just nosed around. I saw small in a relative sense, as compared to its surrounding space. But it was really quite roomy, comfortably furnished, and there was every evidence of people there. The three bedrooms now were small by any yardstick—each contained only a single bed, a chair, a dressing table, small chest of drawers, small closet —hardly more than a cell in a convent—but the sitting room obviously shared by all was outfitted for the usual modern animal comforts, including television and VCR,

hi-fi, racks of magazines, a small desk with electric type-
writer and electronic calculator; it did not look like a movie
set. Something was lacking there still, but I could not put a
finger to it.

I could not find a cellar though I did note a door on the
kitchen wall that could lead to one.

I did not find a laboratory despite the fact that one was
specifically mentioned in the abstracts, and I did not find a
conservatory, also mentioned, unless that referred to the
atrium or entry court.

I did not find a hell of a lot of solace anywhere, to sum
it up.

So I was ready for Bob Alvarez.

I just hoped that he was ready for a formal dinner party
at Pointe House. Naw, naw . . . I knew that he was not.

I went down early on purpose—dressed elegantly casual in
white slacks and silk shirt, simple red cummerbund beneath a navy blazer—ready for anything but hoping for a
spectacular entry by the other guests.

I had also set Alvarez up for an early arrival and I met
him outside beneath the carport.

He glanced me up and down and said, "Shit, man, you
didn't tell me it was black tie."

"No black ties on me, pal," I told him. "But I'll remove
the cummerbund if that would make you more comfortable."

"If I was getting five bills a day, maybe I'd come to
dinner in a cummerbund too," he replied stiffly. "Never
mind, I'm okay." But obviously he was not okay: he
seemed a bit out of it, nervous.

I said, "Relax, these are come-as-you-are dinners, I guess. You'd pass my muster anywhere."

He was gazing around the property as he asked, "Is this ancient man going to be here?"

I said, "Let's hope so. But don't be offended if he does not take sustenance with us. It's been said that nobody ever saw him eat."

Alvarez shivered slightly then gave me a crooked grin. "That's okay. We got people like that in my family too."

I had to ask him, "Would that be among the local Indians?"

He replied almost defiantly: "That's right. My people were on the land when Father Serra came. He took them away from the most beautiful life-style any human could ever have and replaced it with sin and sacrifice."

I said, "Well, that's progress."

Alvarez grinned, said, "Yeah. I'm not bitching. I couldn't go back to the old ways." He chuckled. "I'd miss television and beer too much."

I said, "There you go," and escorted my Indian friend in to formal dinner at Pointe House.

I wanted us to be first on the scene because I had not seen my new friends depart from that first meeting and I was curious to see how they managed it. Remember that I had just shaken down the whole joint, and it had been empty except for Francesca and myself, Hai Tsu and her two helpers.

I took Alvarez into the lounge off the dining room and did honors myself at the bar. He was easy enough to please: half a glass of bourbon lightly diluted with a squirt of seltzer, and he was ready for anything—he thought. We had the place to ourselves for all of five minutes. I had steered Alvarez to a small couch at the wall that afforded us a perfect view of the entire room, also both entrances to it.

"Is Miss Amalie going to be here?" Alvarez wanted to know.

I replied, "Let's hope so."

"Who else besides the ancient man?"

I shrugged, told him, "I was told to expect the same crowd we had last night."

"Who told you that?"

"The housekeeper," I said.

"Miss Ming."

"Yes. But it would distress her to be addressed that way. Call her Hai Tsu."

"Gotcha. So. When are you going to show me how to do that total recall thing? That would be a terrific skill for a police officer."

I said, "Come on. You guys come by that naturally. I never met a cop who ever forgot anything."

He said, "Yes, but *total*—you said even background sounds and odors. That would—"

Alvarez was arrested at midsentence by a background sound that probably he would never forget. We were seated across the room from the piano, situated for the best possible view of the keyboard area. Even that was not too great because of the floor-pedestal music stands grouped beside it. But we could see okay. The big concert grand occupied a corner of the room. There were but two doorways: one leading to the dining room, the other to a hallway at the opposite side; to reach the piano from either one would have to walk directly past our couch.

No one had walked past that couch, and we were the first to arrive. But Valentinius was now at the piano and had just struck up the introductory movement into *Autumn Nocturne*.

Alvarez gave me a dumb look as he asked, "Who's that?"

"That's your ancient man," I told him.

"How'd he get there?" The cop was craning for a discreet look behind the piano.

I said, "Save your eyesight. There are no doors or trick panels back there. Relax. You're going to enjoy this."

"Enjoying it already," Alvarez replied, relaxing back into the cushions with a sigh. "Guy plays like a pro. That how he makes his money?"

"He makes it easier than that I think," I told him.

The music must have been a signal to Hai Tsu and her ladies. The two helpers whisked in and became very busy at the bar. One of them looked up directly into my eyes and seemed a bit startled to find us there, but went on with her chores.

I put a hand on Alvarez and warned him, "Don't look at the girls. Keep watching the piano."

He was saying, "I don't know what—" when again his jaw locked, his eyes flared, and his body stiffened beside me.

In a flash—I mean faster than a fingersnap—the other guests appeared, and I do mean *appeared*. They came in talking a mile a minute, highly energized and having a great time, as though they'd already been partying somewhere else and were instantly transported to the center of this room without even being aware of the transport.

Catherine (the Whore) was the first to spot Alvarez and me. She came swaying over with hand extended, clad in a gown that began off the shoulders and swooped to a vee at the belly button, and her eyes could not get enough of the cop. We stood to greet her and Alvarez stooped to kiss her hand as I introduced them. Her eyes flashed at me above that kiss and she cooed, "Heavens, you gave me a start. I did not see you come in."

Alvarez was stone mute and a little muscle was flicking in his jaw. I am sure I voiced his sentiments exactly as I told Catherine, "You could be no more startled than we. That is a stunning gown, Catherine."

She was looking at Alvarez while replying to that: "Perfectly befitting a whore, would you say?"

The cop's eyes jerked.

I told Catherine, "Perfectly, yes."

Rosary (the Nun) joined us before Alvarez could come unstuck. I introduced them. She squeezed his hand and sweetly informed him, "Yes, I knew your grandfather well. Wonderful man, filled with true Christian humility."

The cop croaked, "He worked at the mission at San Juan Capistrano."

She beamed, replied, "Yes. Dear heart," and went on to the piano.

Catherine urged, "Come sing with us."

"We'll be there," I assured her.

She swept Alvarez with another warm gaze then danced off behind the nun.

Then the others crowded around us and the Chinese

girls were spreading the drinks around as one and all took their turn at Alvarez. He was beginning to look definitely green below the ears and obviously working hard to regulate his breathing—especially when a serving girl placed another bourbon–seltzer in his hand.

As they all trooped off to regroup around the piano, Alvarez leaned in closer to me and took a deep breath. "Jesus Christ!" he whispered.

He was just cussing to release the tension, but I winked and told him, "You may not be too far off at that."

What I was really wondering about though was whether they had been transported to us, or us to them. It was something worth thinking about.

TWENTY-FIVE

And the Angels Sang

This time we had roast suckling pigs, three of them with Chinese apples stuffed into their little mouths, something that probably was squid but could have been anything, several other dishes that looked terrible but tasted great; all in all enough food on that table set for nine to easily feed four times that number. I thought about the abundant life offered by at least one great mystic of the past but still wondered how celestial beings—if indeed these were such—could justify such feasting in a largely hungry world. Jesus of Nazareth always had a ready reply for such criticism of course, so I was not really too hung up on the idea. Anyway, everyone was enjoying it so hugely that I would never voice such thoughts; I was, after all, a guest and eating for free myself.

Even Alvarez found his appetite after the initial shock had worn off, and surprised me by taking seconds around the table and joining spiritedly in the free-flowing conversations. It would be difficult actually to not be drawn in by these people, so gregariously charming, interested and interesting, so full of life and the joyful expression of it.

This was the way it should be, I was thinking, any time people sit down to break bread together; this kind of spirited communion was a celebration of life and went a lot further toward thanks than any hastily mumbled prayer or self-conscious oration to God at the dinner table.

So what the hell—who is to say what angelic is supposed to be?

If I threw a birthday party for my kid, and if he and all his guests spent the whole time solemnly thanking me for my largesse, I'd figure the party was a bust. I'd rather see those kids laughing and playing, having a good time; that would be thanks for me.

I guess that was what Jesus meant.

And certainly these kids at Pointe House wasted no time on solemnity. The banter was equal to anything in Neil Simon's plays and the brilliant diversity of interests was sometimes staggering. These were learned people, and they enjoyed talking about what they knew, but there was no pontificating or preaching at that table, let me assure you.

Alvarez kept throwing me quick grins and nodding his head at things said. Sharp guy, quite a bit better dimensioned than I would have thought, a wide range of interests.

Hilary (the Priest) said something about the *duties* of civilization, and Alvarez chimed in with, "Well sure, we have to carry the torch—right? When it goes out, it's dark around here, and maybe nobody'll know where the matches are."

"Exactly!" Hilary cried. "Enlightment must be ever expanding. When it begins contracting, watch out—watch out!"

Alvarez tossed me a grin as he replied, "The balloon blows up slow but it deflates pretty quick."

"Adolf Hitler wanted to put a match to it," Karl (the Engineer) declared.

"He was a sexual pervert, you know," Catherine remarked.

"But a brilliant mind no less," said John (the Logician). "The pity is that he got so tangled up in those scatterbrained occult movements."

"The Germanens," said Hilary, "were probably responsible for his master race thesis. All that preoccupation with racial purity was insane."

"Not to mention," chimed in Catherine, "the *Fraternitas Saturni*."

"Brotherhood of Saturn," Rosary translated for Alvarez.

"Yes," Catherine said. "I think sex is magical enough as just sex; don't you, Rosary?"

The nun scathingly replied, "Bite your tongue, young lady!" To Alvarez: "The Brotherhood of Saturn should have been called the Brotherhood of Satan. They practiced sexual magic."

"Pardon me, Sister, but I have to go with Catherine," Alvarez told her with a wink at me. "All sex is magical."

Rosary had no ready reply to that. But Pierre (the

Chemist) came in on it at that point. He pointed a finger at Alvarez and said, "I like this man. He says what he thinks, even in the presence of sacred vestments."

Alvarez grinned and told him, "I'm a policeman."

"Indeed!" said Pierre. "Did you hear that, John? A policeman! A weary world cries out for better policemen. I would venture to say that you are a very good policeman, Bob."

Alvarez smiled with a trace of embarrassment and replied, "I try to be. What do you folks know about the body on the beach?"

Apparently no one but me heard that question.

The conversation abruptly turned elsewhere. Alvarez gave me a sheepish grin and helped himself to some more pork, with no effort to get back to the body on the beach. Francesca came in after everyone else had finished the main course, filled her plate, and sat eating silently but attentively as the conversations swirled about her. She gave no notice whatever to Alvarez or to me.

Valentinius again joined us after dessert. He had a brandy, and occasionally joined in the conversation, but spent most of the time in silence, just watching and listening.

Presently, during a lull in the conversation, he gazed directly at Alvarez and told him, "Father Serra did only what he thought was right and holy."

The cop's jaw dropped. He looked at me. I shrugged and shifted my gaze to Valentinius.

"In the name of God," Valentinius continued, "errors are often committed." He raised both hands to shoulder level, smiled at me, dropped them back to the table. "Even in heaven."

I smiled back, told him, "Then maybe I need to revise my ideas about perfection."

"Given enough time," he told me, with twinkling eyes, "all is perfection."

"But in the meantime . . . ?"

"All is error."

I glanced at Francesca, replied to Valentinius, "Interesting concept."

"Error is but perfection in process," he said.

I got the idea that he was enjoying this.

I said, "Sergeant Alvarez is concerned about the error on the beach last night. It's his responsibility to understand what happened."

Alvarez shifted uncomfortably in his chair and gave me a stop-that look but it seemed to bother Valentinius not a whit. He took time to light a cigar, then said to Alvarez, "Your autopsy report should be ready for you now. You should find your responsibilities greatly lightened by it."

Alvarez excused himself and left the room. He was gone for just a couple of minutes during which time Valentinius joined a conversation between Rosary and Catherine —something having to do with the sanctity of sex under the church versus the sanctity of not having sex under the church.

Catherine was saying, "I just don't understand that position. If holy matrimony blesses sex within the church, then why can't you and Hilary have sex? Aren't you united within the church?"

Rosary patiently replied, "I am the Bride of Christ, Catherine!"

"Then why can't you have sex with him? How many brides does he need anyway?"

Rosary turned to their host and sputtered, "Val! Will you tell this . . . this . . . ?"

Valentinius bit down on his cigar and chuckled merrily. He said to Catherine, "For whom or what would you forswear the sexual embrace, my dear?"

"For no body or no thing I've seen yet," she replied soberly.

"So you regard highly this idea of sexual embrace, I take it."

"You take it right."

"Then be happy for your sister that she has found something even more highly to be regarded."

Catherine looked at Rosary with a changing light in the eyes and said, "Okay, maybe I understand that."

"Thank you, dear heart," Rosary said to Valentinius.

He bowed gallantly in his chair and said, "Remember me to your bridegroom."

Catherine said still very soberly, "You know, that's really sweet."

Alvarez returned at that point, his face a study in confusion and bafflement. He sat down and leaned against me to quietly report, "I called in. They'd just received the report. Natural causes, they say. Dead before he hit the beach, they say."

Valentinius was looking at us.

I stared straight back at him and asked, "What killed him?"

He removed the cigar from his mouth and delicately flicked the ashes into a tray as he quietly replied, "What kills us all, Ashton?"

"Error?" I ventured.

"Of course."

"But in this particular instance, this particular error . . . in one so young . . .?"

He puffed on the cigar, glanced at Alvarez, told me, "Sometimes our own error is the most difficult thing to face."

Alvarez growled in a low voice, "Whatever he faced scared hell out of him. That man died in terror."

Valentinius smiled sweetly, asked, "How do you spell that word, Robert? With a T in front of error?"

With that Valentinius flat disappeared.

An instant later we heard him at the piano.

Catherine leapt to her feet and clapped her hands. "Showtime!" she declared happily. "I think tonight I would like to do a striptease."

I doubt that my friend the Indian, Bob Alvarez, even heard that interesting announcement.

He was still staring with open mouth at the vacant chair of our host.

"That man is a devil," he muttered.

I thought of St. Germain, and the distress with which he greeted that same accusation by the old Countess von Georgy at Madame de Pompadour's in the middle eighteenth century.

I leaned closer to Alvarez and whispered to him, "He's playing with us, so play along. And don't worry about the devil. There's no room for him at this inn."

"How do you know that?" Alvarez growled back.

I did not know how I knew, but I knew. Also I had never met the devil so had never experienced him.

"Trust me," I said. "There's no devil here."

Everyone else had gone into the lounge except Francesca. She paused between us and stared at the cop while asking me, "Who is your friend, Ashton?"

Alvarez's jaw wobbled a bit as he reminded her, "We met this morning, Miss Amalie. I'm Sergeant Alvarez."

"Where is your uniform?"

"I, uh . . ." He looked at me for help. I just shook my head and held my peace.

Francesca said, "Do you like the army?"

He replied, humbly, "Yes, Ma'am, I love it."

"That's nice," she said. Then she joined the others in the lounge.

I lit a cigarette and toyed with my coffee. The sergeant of police just sat there, glowering at his hands. The angels in the other room were singing of good times a'coming.

I quietly told my friend the cop, "Stop feeling bad. That's not her."

"Not who?"

"Not the lady you met this morning. I'm sure she knows who you are though, what you are, and why you're here. This one I mean, Francesca II. And she was rubbing at me, not at you. So don't take it to heart."

"Thanks," he said with a tight smile. "I needed that. Even though I don't understand a thing you're talking about."

"Is your case closed?"

"It is not."

"Okay," I said, "so let's go sing with the angels."

He looked toward the lounge, stood up, asked, "That what they are?"

"What do *you* say?"

He smiled and held out a hand to me. "I say let's go sing with the angels. That's nothing new to my family."

I knew that. The American Indians had been communing with the celestials for time out of mind.

Sure, I knew that. And so must Valentinius.

TWENTY-SIX

The Nether Stairs

The superb collection of paintings and sculptures I'd seen the night before in Francesca's studio was now on display in the lounge, but nobody was paying them any attention. All were grouped at the piano singing their heads off and enjoying it immensely.

I gave a nod toward the art display for Alvarez's benefit and told him, "There's the show I saw last night."

He nodded back in understanding and went over to check it out. I was still working at my cigarette and did not wish to blow smoke upon the singers so I trailed along behind Alvarez to get his reaction to the artwork.

He stood for a long moment before a portrait of Francesca—obviously a self-portrait—before commenting, "This is good."

I said, "That, pal, is the understatement of the year. Call it uncanny. Can you figure those colors?"

He gave me a sad smile and replied, "I don't know much about art. But I think it's good." He was moving along the display now, pausing here and there for a closer inspection of those he recognized. "They're all here," he told me a moment later. "Except the ancient man. Where's he?"

I said, "He's everywhere," and looked pointedly at one of the sculptures.

That gave my a friend a start. He moved from one to the other, inspecting several sculptures and then remarking, "They're all alike. I thought they were just decorations for the pictures."

I said, "Maybe so."

He said, "No, no; I don't think so. This means something. It means something to the pictures. Look at this face here now." He was indicating the portrait of John the Ascetic. "Try to see the picture and the statue at the same time. See what I mean?"

I saw what he meant, sure.

My friend the cop was now quickly becoming an art critic, moving interestedly from portrait to portrait and checking out the different angles of view.

I grinned and stepped away from that, then suddenly stopped grinning and walked quickly to the end of the line.

A new portrait was proudly on display there—a double portrait—set slightly apart from the others and bracketed by a pair of Valentinius heads.

Francesca was there and I was there, both of us swirling

from the background of riotous color—but we were not together there; we were merely each present there and juxtaposed within the colors in such a way as to suggest that neither subject could be aware of the other.

It was stunning.

I was still staring at it when Alvarez caught up to me. He reacted with a start too, and stood there beside me without comment until I solicited one.

"What do you think?" I quietly asked him.

"I think she's in love with you," he replied without pause. "It's very obvious, isn't it?"

I said, "Well . . . maybe . . . but how do you get that from the painting?"

He said, "I guess I get it because she put it there. When did you pose for this?"

I said, "Hey, Bob, I didn't pose for this." I put a tentative finger to the edge of the canvas—expecting very, very tacky but encountering entirely dry paint. It was a shock. Oils simply do not dry that fast, not any oils I'd ever encountered before.

Alvarez was saying, "It's the same effect with the ancient man, Ash. I don't understand how that . . ."

Somehow the observation irritated me. Maybe because I did not understand it either—or maybe I simply did not like the effect. Any of it.

I told Alvarez, "Art is illusion, Bob. Francesca herself told me that."

"Maybe so," he said, a bit mournfully, "but I'd say the lady is in love with you. I mean if she painted this. Let's see . . . how would I title it?"

I growled, "Knock it off."

"Soul Mates," he said. "Yeah. I can't compete with that."

This guy was no end of surprises.

I said gruffly, "What th' hell do you know about it, cop?"

He just showed me a sad smile and replied, "I know I can't compete with it."

I had no response to that. I was still staring at the painting in silence when a long moment later Alvarez cleared his throat and said, "Well, I'll leave you to your study. I'm gonna go sing with the angels. Don't, uh, don't go off the deep end here, eh."

I muttered, "Thanks. I'm fine, Bob."

He walked away, joining the others in song as he approached them.

I certainly did not feel like singing.

I did not know what I felt like at that moment. A bit sad, I think, an almost mournful sadness—no, different than that—more subtle—disappointment . . . or some sort of wistful . . .

I did know that I had seen enough of that painting, for the moment anyway. It had a very disturbing effect on me. I was standing near the hallway door so I roused myself from that depressing whatever I was falling into and just stepped on through and found my way around to the kitchen. From there I could hear the Chinese girls busily clearing the dinner table in the dining room. The kitchen was clear. I went through to the door I'd noted earlier during my inspection of the house, tried it, found it unlocked, entered.

There was, yeah, a cellar.

I found a light switch at the head of the stairs and counted twenty steps as I descended. It was very neat and tidy down there, stone walls, stone flooring, evidently a pantry area and wine cellar combined. Really did not know what I was looking for. Well, yes, I guess I did. Because I found it: another door set flush into the stone and barely noticeable behind a stand of wine racks.

It featured a trick pivot like the one in the elevator pit. Two square flashlights—similar to the navy's battle lanterns—were affixed to a rough rock wall just inside. I took one down and tried it. It worked and the battery seemed fully charged. Another long flight of stairs invited me downward.

Devils, eh?

I didn't know about that.

But I had the very eerie feeling that maybe I was descending into the pits of hell . . . while the angels sang—upstairs.

The concept of heaven being located *up* there and hell *down* there is probably as old as man himself. But that view is tied in very closely to early man's model of reality. Even the enlightened Greeks of Plato's time still used the mythical cosmology derived from the much earlier Sumerians and Babylonians, whose model of reality divided existence into the spheres of celestial air, celestial water, and a crystal celestial fortress which floats in the celestial water and in which is embedded the physical world which man inhabits.

This was a very small world.

The crystal celestial fortress (or sphere) of Sumerian–Babylonian legend is divided into twelve zodiacal parts. Within the sphere, which rather looks like a round bowl with a transparent dome, the waters of the Bitter Lake fill the bowl and support the earth's disk (which is flat) beneath the dome, which is filled with celestial air.

The Babylonians believed that their Ziggurat, the Tower of Babel, was situated in the precise center of the celestial sphere, so that all of the created world radiated out from that center.

As I said, it was a very small world.

Above the Ziggurat is stacked the vault of the sky, divided into three parts; below lies the city of the dead, which is surrounded by seven walls containing within them the dwelling places of the inhabitants of those nether regions.

The Greeks of course decided that Mount Olympus occupied the precise center of the universe. They still had the earth as a disk floating upon the bitter (salt) waters. The Mediterranean flowed in through the Strait of Gibralter (Pillars of Hercules) at the extreme western edge of the disk, almost splitting the world into two equal parts with the continents of Europe, Africa, and Asia grouped about it.

That was the whole universe, pal, even for the Greeks.

They put Hades, the Underworld, in the far west where the sun sinks into the sea. But this too was a nether region inhabitated by spooks and demons, and there was no way there save by Charon's ferry.

It may be interesting to consider that the Greeks of Plato's time would have regarded North and South America, if they'd found it, as Hades. More interesting though is the realization that on the surface of a sphere, any stretch toward any direction—north, east, south, or west—is also a stretch downward: down under, as we regard Australia today; the other side of the sphere is the nether region.

Neither the Sumerians, the Babylonians, the Stone Age Greeks or any other early people actually believed that hell was a hole in the ground. They simply had no conceptual basis for such an idea. Indeed man became man during the eternal winter of the last great ice age, and those who survived to emerge into the true dawn of mankind did so by and large because they had found comforting refuge from the cold within the greatly hospitable Mother Earth, in her nether regions of perfect ambient temperature control.

Man became man as dwellers of the underworld.

Would he forget so soon his origins, and learn to fear them as the habitat of spooks and demons?

I think not. So I prefer to believe that the early mythical cosmology never intended to so characterize the womb of mankind. I believe they knew, or had been told somehow, that their model of the universe was seriously deficient and that other peoples on other lands existed beyond the Pillars of Hercules. They accounted for this knowledge through their mythologies, wondrous tales of the imagination designed to describe the indescribable—or the inexperienced.

That is my belief now and it was my belief on that night

at Pointe House as I descended the nether stairway of the angels.

So why was I so damned spooked by the possible presence of demons?

It's in the genes I guess . . . in the genes. And mine were crying like a babe in the darkness alone.

TWENTY-SEVEN

Bodies Immortal

The descent was by curving stairway cut into a smooth stone wall—and by smooth I mean like polished marble or heavy glass. The darkness was so absolute at the top of that journey that the beam cast by the flashlight defined only a narrow cone of reality for my senses to focus on, producing a vertigolike effect and encouraging me to maintain sensory contact with one hand along the wall during that early descent. I had the distinct sensation though of descending around the sides of a large round hollow—not a narrow passageway twisting downward but rather like being inside a large vessel and spiraling slowly downward along its inner walls.

I recall reflecting upon the fact that my guiding hand upon the wall encountered no seams or flaws of any kind to interrupt that smooth texture. I have no idea how deep the descent. I paused at several points to cast the beam of light about in attempts to gauge the dimensions of the chamber, but could see nothing beyond the few steps below and above my route and a few yards of the wall that provided it.

Again though—as earlier with Francesca—I began to note the subtle change in atmosphere as I continued the descent. It was definitely warmer and the air pure and almost sweet in the nostrils. I even noted that my breathing became easier. Shortly thereafter I began coming into the light; very pale at first, then growing steadily until suddenly all was light; not the kind in which you stand blinking for adjustment but an all-encompassing kind of light that is bright white yet softly illuminating and *does not cast shadows*.

And I was definitely in a different kind of place.

It was a huge chamber, yes—I think—and totally filled with that strange light—yet I could not see the ends of it.

It appeared to be some sort of technological facility, though not of any technology I'd ever experienced. This was nothing at all like the mission control center I'd dreamed about. There were no people, no gadgets or machinery—but a sort of tinkling sound seemed to faintly fill the whole place—remember the wind chimes I mentioned earlier when Francesca and I found the access to the tidal cave?—like that, only a bit louder and constant, and I had the feeling that the sound was somehow associated with whatever this place was about.

I call it a place for lack of a better word.

But it was more than a place; it was an experience involving the whole mind and the whole body. I was aware that something that is essentially me was somehow, in some way, responding to something present there within that experience, but I have never come to any better understanding than that. I just knew that this was technology rather than spiritology—and that whatever the nature of my response, it was at least 99 percent a this-world response wholly within time and space.

It was not a city, or a dwelling, or a craft of any kind that I could understand—but then how would a cockroach describe to his friends his first venture from the musty darkness into a modern human kitchen with its fluorescent lights, gleaming tiles, electronic digital gadgets, and wide flowing spaces? What would be his point of reference? No point whatever, that's right; and there was no point of reference or relativity for me either within that place.

Certainly I no longer needed the flashlight. It seems like I would have turned it off at some point when it was no longer needed, but I do not recall doing so, nor do I remember the transition from stairway to place. I just know that suddenly there I was in the light, everything that is me vibrating to some strange new quality to existence, being drawn almost magnetically deeper into the light.

Then suddenly I saw Hai Tsu, a somehow different kind of Hai Tsu. She was naked, and her body was like some denser *concentration* of the light, almost incandescent, yet I could see through it. She was about ten paces ahead of me but when she spoke it was like speaking inside my head instead of from her position outside of me.

"A thousand pardons, Ash Shen, but you must not be here."

"Where is here, Hai Tsu?"

"Here is where you must not be, my master. How do I forbid you? Yet I must. Go back, please."

"I cannot go back without understanding."

"You would understand the understanding that is not yours to know? Please, do not command me in this."

I am not relating a dream here. This happened, exactly as I am giving it.

And then Valentinius happened.

He "appeared in glory" beside Hai Tsu—much more physically substantial than she—in whole body I mean, but that body was shooting light just like hers.

His words occurred through my ears, not inside the head like Hai Tsu's. "We must respect her imperatives, Ashton."

"*We* must?"

"To be sure. I, no less than you."

It occurred to me then—just popped into the head; I don't know from where—but I had to ask: "She is one of the Immortals?"

"In the way we think of it, yes."

"How 'bout the way she thinks of it?"

"She was sent to serve, Ashton. But not to reveal."

"That is her imperative? To not reveal?"

"One of them, to be sure. You must not challenge it."

"Is this the real Hai Tsu then? This . . . *light*?"

"There is no unreal Hai Tsu," he told me. "All that you see is very real."

"What is this place, Valentinius?"

He replied, "It has been called The Isle. But of course it is not an island, not as you would think of it."

"The Isle of the Immortals," I guessed.

"It has been so characterized. But now, please, we distress our hostess. We must depart."

I said, "Wait!" and spoke directly to Hai Tsu: "Why would you choose to live forever like this? You are a ghost serving ghosts! What is the point?"

She replied in my head: "The greatest joy is to serve. Hai Tsu very happy. Sometimes, Ash Shen, least is most and most is least."

That sentiment sounded a bit familiar. I think Jesus said it though maybe not just that way.

She was at me again. "Please, you must go. Danger here. Not just for Ash Shen, but danger for his servant too. Please go back."

Valentinius stretched out a hand to me, said, "Come, Ashton."

It was not a self-volitional movement—I mean, I did not decide to do that; I simply obeyed: I stepped forward and took his hand and heard myself singing "The Whiffenpoof Song" at the top of my lungs in company with all my friends at the piano. There was no sensation of moving through space or time, dimensional barriers, or anything else; I was just suddenly there beside Valentinius on the piano seat.

So . . . did all that really happen?

You can bet my ass it happened.

I still had the flashlight clutched tightly in my other hand, and it was still shining brightly.

Francesca was now beside Valentinius at the piano and they were entertaining with a four-hand exercise at the keyboard. I'd made a quick break for the bar and had my

Scotch—rocks firmly in one hand and the blazing flashlight inanely in the other when Alvarez made it over to me and accusingly asked me, "How the hell did you do that?"

He looked like hell, all wild in the eyes and several different shades of color mottling his face.

"Do what?" I asked, still a bit dazed myself.

He growled, "The same thing these other people did. I was standing with Miss Amalie not two feet from that piano when you just suddenly showed up there beside the ancient man. Jesus Christ, I hope I never have to testify to any of this in court!"

I said in a rather weak voice, "Simmer down, there's a perfectly sane explanation for all this. I'll share it with you as soon as I find it."

The cop said, "Yeah, sure you will. You're a hypnotist, huh. You caught me off guard and put this whammy on me. Now I'm—"

I said, "Wish I was that good a hypnotist, pal, but I am not. If you think you've been abused, you should have been with me just now."

He said, "Just tell me how you did that!"

I said wearily, "I didn't do it, had nothing to do with it, was nowhere around here. I was outside somewhere, downside somewhere, clear out of the house, far away. Valentinius came and took my hand and—"

"Bullshit! He was right here the whole time you were gone, what d'you mean he took your hand?—he was play-ing the goddamn piano and the rest of us were singing and . . . and . . ."

I said, "Remind me to tell you about bilocation when we have more time. How long was I gone?"

"Gone? *Gone*? Man, I think you're still gone. What're you doing with that fucking flashlight? What d'you think you are, a fucking miner or something? I leave you looking at the picture and the next I know you're—will you turn that damned thing off?—next I know you're singing "poor little lambs" with us with that fucking flashlight!"

I muttered, "Hey keep it down . . . the ladies."

"Ladies, hell," he growled, but he did glance around and lower his voice. "That woman really did do a striptease; I mean . . . I never saw it done that way before!"

I said, "Ah well, it's only bodies celestial so what the hell. Or maybe bodies immortal; still what the hell. Take these Chinese girls now, they have—"

"Come on, Ash. Cut the bullshit, will you. Where'd you go? And how'd you get back here that way?"

I replied, "Would you believe that I visited the Isle of the Immortals?"

The cop said, "Right now, I would not believe a damned thing you told me."

"Think back," I said. "Remember a time when you were a little boy on your grandpappy's knee and he's telling you stories his grandpappy told him about the Golden Ones, the Great Ones who came from far across the sea in great, shining canoes that captured the sun and gave birth to the moon and all the stars in the heavens."

Alvarez was giving me an odd look. He slid onto a bar stool and rested his chin on a balled first, very quietly said, "You did hypnotize me, huh. I don't remember telling you anything about that."

"Didn't have to tell me," I replied. "The story has been told in many variations from Cape Horn to Alaska, even on

Easter Island and throughout the archipelagoes of the Pacific. This was the only way those ancient peoples could relate the mind-blowing visitations by a highly advanced race who came to instruct and enlighten. It found its way into Chinese legend as the Way of the Tao and the Isle of the Immortals, into Egyptian lore as the Isle of Isis and Atlantis. It's the Mount Olympus of the Greeks and it's the Roman Pantheon, and I believe it to be the source of all mankind's early wisdom and the first intimations of immortality."

"Are you trying to tell me how you did that?"

I replied, "No, I am trying to tell you what did me. But I think we'd better wait for that. I think we may be approaching the moment of crisis, and I want to get ready for that."

"You hypnotized me, huh."

I said, "I'm trying to unhypnotize you, pal. You've got to get it together. Because I think I may really need your help before this night is done."

He sighed, looked around the big room, said, "I think it's already done for me. I'm ready to bail out of here."

I could appreciate that.

Fifty-one percent of me wanted to do the same thing.

But I knew that I had to see the night through.

One does not, I say again, defy the angels. And clearly I was the man for Valentinius.

TWENTY-EIGHT

The Show Goes On

As by some hidden signal, the jolly partying came to an end and all the characters save Francesca moved to a solemn inspection of the art display. She stood haughtily removed from all that, arms folded at the breast and eyes directed stonily upward to the wall above.

I had a flash then—a genuine burst of understanding—about Francesca and that art.

I left Alvarez steeped in thought at the bar—thought, I took it, aimed at Francesca herself because he was staring a hole through her. I realized of course that the guy had seemed fascinated by the lady from their first meeting; I had taken it as a romantic interest; now I was not so sure about that.

Anyway I corralled the lady and strong-armed her into a walk-through of the improvised gallery, she protesting all the way in terms not especially complimentary to me or my ancestry. But I forced her to look, and to discuss the style and technique of several of the paintings until I could confirm my hunch and play the only hand I'd decided I had to play.

"You did not paint these," I told her.

She bristled, said, "Of course I painted them. Do you think they came from the blue?"

I said, "Maybe. But you are not the master. This work did not come from Francesca II. That's the real secret about you, isn't it. The other Francesca, the working Francesca, the daytime Francesca who experiences only slight intimations of *this* Francesca, *she* is the master."

She responded with haughtiness, "Whatever are you talking about, Mr. Ford."

I told her, "We're going to discuss another painting; come on." I dragged her to the double portrait dubbed Soul Mates by my art critic friend, the cop, demanded: "Tell me about this one."

She sniffed, looked at the floor, replied, "It captures neither of us. I am ashamed of this painting."

"Then why do you display it as the crown of the show?"

"Did I do that?" She looked around, seemed to be losing herself, leaned against me, said very quietly: "Help me, Ashton. I need to come out."

This was, yeah, Francesca I coming out.

I held her in my arms and *kissed* her out of there, then commanded: "Stay here! Don't let her back! She is trying to undermine you!"

The voice was weak but steady as she replied, "Yes, I . . . I think I understand."

This is shivery stuff, understand.

Maybe it does not read that way, and you have to experience it directly to get the full effect of it, but believe me I was shivering inside. Ask any psychiatrist who works with multiple personalities.

I looked up and saw Alvarez hovering nearby. I caught his eye; he came on over. "Know what's happening?" I asked him.

He jerked his head in an understanding nod. "Some of it, I think. Can I help?"

I turned her over to his willing arms and I told him, "Keep her engaged. Discuss the paintings with her, anything, but keep this personality present."

Alvarez understood, yes, quite a bit more than I would realize he understood until some time later. He took over without missing a beat, and I went to talk with Valentinius.

The old soul was giving me one of his patented wise looks as I approached him; he knew I was coming; knew why I was coming.

Before I could get a word out, he said to me, "Good work, Ashton. And just in time. We must depart soon. Hai Tsu has been ordered home. We must leave before her."

I probably already knew or guessed the answer, but I said, "Why?"

He ignored it, told me instead: "All abodes are temporary after all. You will not need the paper I gave you. Perhaps it will be useful however if you should wish to clean up a bit behind us."

I felt suddenly very humbled; looked around the magnificent room and the palatial furnishings; told him, "I am sorry I failed you, Valentinius."

"Ah, but you have not failed me, my brother," he said generously. "I did not ask you here to rescue the abode. Another shall be found, when it is needed." He smiled. "Perhaps not for another hundred years, as you reckon it."

I asked, "What's it all about, brother?"

He smiled. "But you already know that, don't you. Never mind, it shall come to you in time." His gaze shifted to the exhibition and those grouped there in almost worshipful appreciation. "They are joyful, are they not? Because they are filled with the secret. Francesca's secret, and yours. Ah, yes. They are joyful."

I said, working very hard at a thought, "Valentinius . . . is this what I think it is? Are all these people . . . ?"

He replied, "They are coming into understanding, yes."

I said, "But . . . I always thought it would be . . . like . . . instantaneous."

He explained, "If you board a plane in San Francisco, go promptly to sleep, awaken in New York—are you any wiser when you wake than when you fell asleep?"

I said, "Well . . ."

"But if instead of sleeping on the plane, if instead you bring a briefcase stuffed with work to be studied—say for a business conference at the end of the journey—do you arrive in New York wiser than you were when you left San Francisco?"

I said, "See what you mean, yeah. These folks are catching up on their studies."

"This folk," he corrected me.

I said, "Oh shit."

It was not exactly the understanding I'd been reaching for, but it reached me instead.

I tried it on him. "These people are all pieces of you?"

He said, "Oh no"—chuckled—"Dear me, no, not pieces of *me*, Ashton. Never mind, do not be embarrassed. You will understand when understanding is needed. Something else is more directly bothering you, I see. Hai Tsu is bothering you. Do not be bothered for Hai Tsu. She is not called home in disgrace but in recognition of admirable service."

I asked, "Where is that home? Lemuria, Mu, Atlantis, Isis; by whatever name, where is home for Hai Tsu?"

He laughed, told me, "You very nearly stumbled into it, my brother. At the very edge of infinity one could say."

I said, "I thought infinity could have no edges. The infinite is unbounded, isn't it, so what's with edges?"

He replied, "Infinity is both bounded and unbounded, edged and unedged. How would one define space and time beyond the lip of a black hole, eh? Both space and time become infinite, mass and energy become infinite, infinity itself finds new infinities within itself. Is infinity not also present at the outer edge of the black hole? So what is that infinity within the hole?"

I told him, "You left me back there at the lip, my friend."

He laughed again, apparently enjoying the little exchange. "Consider then that the black hole is not fixed in the panoply of heaven. It moves as do all existent things. Think of that, eh? A portable infinity?"

I cried, "Damn! Right here inside this mountain!"

"Do not leap at truth that way, Ashton. It may leap away from you in consternation." But I could see by his reaction that I'd leapt a bit closer than he intended me to. "Suffice to understand that there is room in our infinity for Hai Tsu and her infinity, but that you in present form could not survive hers."

"So how does she survive ours?"

"Ah, but that is one of her imperatives you see."

"And that is why she was called home." I'd already decided.

He replied, "Well . . . but not in disgrace."

I said, "In discretion."

"You could put it that way."

I told him, "I saw something strange in another chamber earlier today. Looked like steel tubes or cylinders fused into solid rock, work tables made of the same stuff. What . . . ?"

He showed me his hands at shoulder level. "Obviously a work room of some sort."

"The cylinders . . ." I persisted.

"Well . . ." He smiled. "Even a portable infinity must have its portability, eh? No. Do not think of them as engines." Guy was reading my mind, right off the top. "I fear there is no correlation in this language. Think of ionization chambers however and you will be closer than engines."

I asked him, "What's going to happen to this mountain when they blast out of there?"

He laughed again. "There shall be no blasting out, Ashton. Oh no. The effect shall be very subtle."

I was feeling like a first-grader trying to get the drift of a doctoral thesis on creation theory. So maybe I was reaching for more comfortable ground when I changed that subject to ask my mentor, "What did you expect me to do with that power of attorney?"

"Oh well, you see . . . there had been a betrayal, Ashton. The careful work of centuries was being undone for greed and—"

"Why didn't you tell me all this right up front?" I asked almost angrily. "Maybe I could have approached the thing from a better angle and—"

"No no, Ashton, you have not grasped the central problem. You have done precisely as I hoped you would. The paper was designed purely to put you in touch with the situation and to forestall, if necessary, any interference with the work to be done here. The work I would say is now in its final hour—and you have already done that which needed doing, by a hand such as yours, with an understanding such as yours, with a heart such as yours. Do you see now?"

I thought I was seeing, yes.

I told Valentinius, "It all has been for Francesca."

"Yes."

"She needed me to . . ."

"Yes, go on, follow it through."

"She had lost herself. You hoped I would help her find herself. Before . . ."

"Yes, before . . . ?"

"Before she arrived in New York."

"Precisely! Oh I am delighted with you, my brother."

I said, "But it really isn't over yet, is it?"

He replied, "Well there may be a final detail awaiting some small resolution. I shall be depending upon you, Ashton, to do in your heart what you know must be done. As with my old friend, Tom."

I said, feeling a sudden queasiness, "Uh huh. So why don't you tell me about old friend Tom."

"He was betrayed by his own flesh. What else must I say?"

I replied, "Like, uh, how difficult it is to confront one's own errors? Tom could not confront Jim's errors?"

"Oh he confronted them. And saw in them the seeds within himself. Tom also, you see, though a good man and staunch friend, was not above small betrayals."

I really did not want to discuss that matter any longer. I didn't want to discuss anything whatever in fact. I was beginning to feel sick in the stomach; I knew that I was not going to like what lay directly ahead in this night.

But I knew too that I could not or would not do a thing to alter it.

I left my angel standing there and went over to collect Francesca.

At least, I thought, I would get her out of there before the walls came tumbling down.

But I was wrong about that too as you shall see.

CHAPTER TWENTY-NINE

From the Heart

I don't know if I have made it sufficiently clear at this point that I was very much in love with Francesca. That may sound a big gratuitous considering the brevity of the relationship—and I have already told you that I had never put much store in the idea of love at first sight—nevertheless, all that notwithstanding, things of the heart often defy logic or rationalization—and if I had resisted the idea in the beginning, certainly I surrendered to it entirely during that episode in the tidal cave.

It is possible too, I believe, to be crazy in love and not immediately know that you are, especially if those moments are crowded with cross-purposes as mine had been during that furious pace of events during the thirty-odd hours that I had known Francesca.

Whatever...I was very deeply in love and knew it at

this time, and I was strongly disturbed over the implications of my little talk with Valentinius. I still did not understand as much as I would have liked to understand, feeling mainly a vague sense of danger or impending loss. Bear in mind too that I was fairly reeling from the astounding revelations that had been pouring in on me—and there did not seem to be the luxury of time available for me to sit down and skull the thing through toward the best possible resolution.

I admit it: I was just riding along with the thing and trying to keep some balance while doing so—all the while feeling like a surfer atop a killer wave rushing toward the rocks.

Valentinius was very adroit at concealing truths within truths as he spoke. Angels do not lie, do they? I would think not. But there are ways to tell the truth and still achieve the same effect as a lie. So I was not at all sure as to where I stood in relation to the truth, where Francesca stood, where anything concerning this house stood.

I knew only that I wanted to get her out of there. No discredit to Valentinius intended; I had done a bit of work with the mentally disturbed before and knew how very delicate could be the catharsis in schizophrenia of the type being suggested by Francesca's behavior. Angels maybe are better at this sort of thing than anyone, but still I think I would have preferred to have a second opinion with medical credentials behind it. Whatever the work or goal of this assembly at Pointe House, I did not feel that it should be regarded as a life or death matter for the woman I loved . . . or for any mortal for that matter. I always figured that heaven could wait for the dispositions on earth; what else does heaven have to do after all? We down here are the ones with the time problem.

So call me dumb or insensitive or overreactive or whatever; I was doing what I think any sane man would do in the circumstances: I wanted to get my love out of that insanity.

She still seemed a bit confused, not exactly sure where she was and what was happening, but she was intelligently discussing the paintings with Alvarez and seemed to be maintaining a grip on her own identity. One of her problems I think was that she did not recognize those others present—or maybe she did and that was causing the confusion, because she kept looking from John the Ascetic to his painting while discussing it with Alvarez.

I stepped up behind them and put an arm on her, asked her, "Do you remember painting that?"

She encircled my waist with an arm and drew close, like a little girl seeking comfort from Daddy as she replied, "Oh yes, I remember it well, but I didn't realize that I was painting from memory. I thought it just *came* to me. Several of these, Ash—look at these down here . . ." She was pointing toward the canvases of Karl and Catherine. She glanced about and located the real subjects. "See, these are actual people. And I'm *sure* I've never seen—oh well, maybe I could have if . . ."

I said, "It's okay. How would you like to get out of here for a while?"

She gave a weak smile to Alvarez and said, "The sergeant just suggested the same thing a moment ago. Are you guys taking turns, drawing lots, or what?"

Alvarez turned beet red.

I tried to cover for him, telling her, "Well Bob is prettier than me, but I'm more constant. Don't ever date a cop, Francesca, unless you need a ticket fixed or he first introduces you to his mom. On second thought maybe Bob is the exception. He titled your double portrait Soul Mates."

She smiled at him and said, "How nice. That's my title too."

He gruffly said, "That's what I figured."

I told him, "I think we really should get her out of here. Something's going down, and I don't like the smell of it."

He said, "Me neither. Any time you're ready, I'm ready."

But Valentinius obviously was not ready.

He joined us, smiling all around, took Francesca's hand and said to her, "It is time for the unveiling, my dear."

I quickly said, "Val . . . wait . . . can we put this off a while? I'd like to—"

"It requires but a moment," he demurred. "Do not hasten to judgment, dear Ashton. It is the moment we have all been working toward. Trust your heart, my brother."

"How old are you, sir?" Alvarez ventured bluntly.

"As old as the hairs on your grandfather's grandfather, my son, and then some," Valentinius replied without breaking smile.

"Somehow you just don't look it," the cop growled.

"Thank you," said the angel. "Nor do I feel it. Now look, the exhibition is ready and we shall down with the veils."

He led us all to the opposite wall and positioned Francesca where she had the full exhibition in view.

John the Ascetic stood beside his portrait, Hilary and

Pierre, Karl and Rosary and Catherine beside theirs, solemn in their sacred duty and staring at Francesca with an expression I could characterize only as transcending love. That accounted for only six of the forty or so portraits, but subtle changes were occurring in those others—it was happening right before our astonished eyes and Alvarez was holding his breath again.

I said, "Francesca, don't—"

"Now now," said the angel, his tone lightly chastising. "This is Francesca's moment, Ashton. Let her have it."

He stepped back to stand about midway between Francesca and the exhibit, smiling with approval and reassurance and love and God I don't know what all was in that smile, but I suddenly lost all reservations about the thing.

Francesca gave me an uncertain look. I nodded reassuringly and smiled at her.

All the paintings had changed subtly.

It was obvious now that all depicted the same subject.

The subject was Francesca herself.

Even John and Hilary, Pierre and Karl—they too were now Francesca.

Suddenly I knew why.

Francesca took a tentative step forward. In a strangled little voice she asked, "What does this mean, Father Medici?"

He replied, "The veils are down, my dear. Go to yourself."

"But . . ." She took a step closer. "All are myself."

"Go to the all then my dear."

She cried, "Ohhhh!" and I feared for an instant that she

would faint, but then she quickly reasserted herself and looked back at me.

I was absolutely rooted to my spot, could not move, could hardly breathe.

Valentinius went over to stand inside the exhibit, held out a hand to her, said, "Come."

She looked uncertainly from him to me, and I knew what she was up against; this guy had raised a hand to me a short while earlier and said "come" and I had gone like a robot at his command.

But this was not a command.

There was a decision to be made here, and only Francesca herself could make it; I understood that.

She cried, "Ashton! Help me!"

I sent her all my love and adoration in a look that perhaps would have to last an eternity and told her, "I release you, Francesca. Do as you must."

I heard it in my head from the angel: "Good, good! Thank you, brother."

She had turned and was walking toward them.

There was a strange shift or something in the fabric of that room; the walls seemed to dissolve, and the whole scene in front of me was like suspended in celestial air. The whole thing was shrinking, receding into the distance so that when Francesca reached Valentinius and turned back to look at me, it was as though from a great distance.

The whole company—the entire cast of characters— were smiling at me, and there was triumph in those smiles, though perhaps triumph tinged with a touch of pathos.

The picture kept receding until it was a mere point away off into nowhere—but just before that moment, a fleeting second before that moment, there was some sort of shift and all the figures except Valentinius blended together into a single image, then that image blended with Valentinius and collapsed into nothingness, and then the fabric restored itself—time and space reasserted its domain and raised the walls—and Alvarez and I were alone in the room.

The cop was thunderstruck. He cried, "Good God, where'd she go?"

I said, "Home I guess," and put a hand to my face to conceal the tears.

But she'd gone farther than that I think.

I believe that my soul mate had just returned to the One.

Alvarez was walking the outside wall in a daze, probing it with both hands and tossing me an occasional quick look as though to maintain touch with something real. The paintings were gone, the heads were gone, all was gone as though it had never existed—and maybe it had not in this particular corner of reality.

Hai Tsu appeared before me then with her handmaidens, and all were naked bodies of light.

I noted poor Alvarez as he clapped a hand to his head and slid down the wall to seat himself on the floor, peering fearfully at the apparitions that stood between him and me.

Hai Tsu spoke within my head to tell me, "Time is come, Ash Shen, to say good-bye. Please remember this servant with love."

I answered the same way, telling her, "Thank you Hai Tsu. In truth you are not the servant but the mistress of the court. I regret that I have caused you distress. I could never forget you, and all my memories will touch you with love. Bon voyage, my sister."

That electric body was pulsing with unrestrained joy as it dimmed and faded and disappeared. The other two remained behind for one electric second, darted to either end of the great room as though taking a last look around, then they too winked out.

Poor Alvarez wailed "Jesus Christ!" from his side of the room and began crawling toward me.

I went to help him—though Lord knows I needed some help myself—and I told him, "You may not be too far off at that, my son."

"Don't you start it!" he growled, then he flopped onto his back and laughed his way back to sanity.

I recommend laughter as a good antidote for terror, but terror was not my problem and I did not feel like laughing.

I sat down on the floor beside my friend, the cop, and wept as he laughed.

I recommend tears as a good antidote for sorrow.

And I guess I was about the sorriest bastard you would ever care to meet.

It is I think entirely possible to die of a broken heart.

THIRTY

Casefile Wrap-Up

Everything was gone—the booze, the food, even the dirty dishes were gone. I left Alvarez recovering on the floor from his laughing fit and went to check the rest of the house. And, yeah, all that was gone too—all the stuff from my suite except the stuff I'd brought in the overnight kit and the freshly cleaned clothing I'd worn down from Malibu. The other suites had been cleaned out too; there was nothing left, not even lint to mark the scene with evidence of human habitation.

Francesca's studio was clean as a whistle—not a canvas or brush or dab of paint, no modeling clay or framing or tools of any kind to mark her sojourn there.

I ran outside to check the cottages and, yeah—deserted, abandoned—the entire habitation had vanished like the last rays of light from a dead bulb; there was not even an odor of life left behind.

I paused at the carport as I came back to the house, wondering what was disturbing me there—then realized that Francesca's VW was missing.

I went on inside and up to the lounge. Alvarez was just hanging up the phone. He seemed to have himself in hand again. He told me, "I called the hospital. They say Miss Amalie died a few minutes ago."

I was not that much in hand myself yet.

I snarled at him, "What the hell are you talking about?"

He said, "Give me one of your damned coffin nails, will you?"

I gave him a cigarette and took one for myself, lit them both, glared at him, said, "What's this about a hospital?"

He said, "Okay, I haven't been entirely up-front with you."

I said, "Sorry, I can't really believe that coming from an officer of the law."

He said, "Okay, I deserve that. Just remember that I've been investigating a very weird situation. Knew it was weird soon as I saw her car. It—"

"It's missing," I told him. "Everything is missing, gone, kaput. Nothing is here, pal, but you and me. And I'm not sure about me."

He brushed that aside to say, "I assisted a traffic investigation last year. Little VW bug lost it on a bad curve in the canyon. It's sitting right now in the storage yard of a body shop, waiting disposition. Torn to shit. I mean totaled in any sense of the word. The driver got pretty nearly totaled too. Never regained consciousness, been in a coma all this part year. Well she lost her coma a few minutes ago. Francesca Amalie was just declared officially dead by the resident on duty at Irvine."

I thought I had already bottomed out, but I suddenly found a new bottom of despair. I said to Alvarez, "Let me get this straight . . ."

"Knew something was weird when I saw that VW parked out there this morning. Exact duplicate, except this one wasn't torn up. I checked my notes from the accident investigation. Even the license tags checked out. I went down to the body shop after I left here this morning to see if the wreck was still there. It was. But, see, I figured some kind of game, especially when she gave me her name and background this morning. I thought, shit, what scam is this? I thought I'd seen 'em all. I hadn't seen the victim since right after the accident, and she was all in bandages then. So I went to Irvine again this morning and I saw her, and shit it was the same face except maybe a little wasted from a year in coma."

I found strength somewhere to feel sympathy for the guy. I told him, "You've had a rough day."

"Say that again, friend. Then when I found the guy at Newport wearing the same death mask as the guy on the beach here, well then I figured . . . shit, I didn't know what to figure. So when you called and invited me to dinner, I ran all the way here."

I said, "And then it really started getting rough."

"Amen to that, amen and amen. You say the VW is not down there now?"

"That's where it's not," I replied. "It was another part of

the set, and it's been broken down and packed up and taken away in the same bag as the rest of the set. None of this stuff was real, not any of it."

He said, "Now wait a minute . . ."

I said, "You may as well just buy it and save yourself a lot of mental strain. The stuff never existed, at least not in *this* domain. Where was Francesca living at the time of the accident?"

He withdrew a notebook, flipped through it, found the entry he sought, told me, "She shared a loft with three other girls down in town, near the pottery shack."

I said, "Okay, that checks. She told me—*some*body told me that she was living there when Valentinius approached her and brought her here. Come to think of it though, she was a bit vague about that."

"Wait a minute. You said none of it existed. Now you're talking like it did."

I said, "*She* existed, Bob. *All* of the people existed. Still do somewhere, but, shit, don't ask me where. That bit about Valentinius commissioning her to do a portrait though—that sounds like dream stuff. He came for her while she was in coma after the accident."

Alvarez said, "Stop that."

I said, "Bullshit; look at it, man. It's what this whole thing has been about. Francesca must have been something pretty terrific to rate that kind of attention from Valentinius. That guy is not just an angel; he's an *arch*angel. He—"

"Yeah, but I thought the angels come after you're already dead. Shit, it looks to me like he was helping her die or something; what the hell kind of wings is that? That's interference, that's...it should be against the rules; I could get an indictment on that guy from a grand jury. That's incitement to suicide, it's...it's..."

I said, "Argue with an archangel if you want to, pal, but leave me out of it."

"Well, goddammnit, you didn't do much better for yourself. I swear you told her to go ahead and die."

God damn but that hit me hard, true though it was. I guess Alvarez saw it on my face because he quickly tried to take it back. "I mean how could you have known?—it's my fault for holding out on you."

I said very wearily, "It's nobody's fault, Bob. How could you have seen what you saw and still want to indict someone for it?"

He was silent for a moment, then replied, "Guess you're right. It *was* something terrific, wasn't it. I think I want to go that way. With the ancient man showing me the way."

I growled, "Better clean up your act then. And don't really bank on Valentinius, even then. This was quite a bit more than a mere death escort you know. This was a total reintegration within the flesh. Before death of the body occurred, I mean. Maybe that is what many comas really are. Takes a while to work it all out sometimes. Especially with a very old soul. You saw all those paintings. Forty or more. Each one was a piece of Francesca."

Alvarez shivered. He said, "You mean, like reincarnations?"

I shrugged and replied, "However you prefer to look at it. The point is the total personality was reintegrated within the flesh. They have a name for that in most of the mystery religions, even in Christianity, though each call it some-thing different."

"What do *you* call it?" Alvarez said wonderingly.

"I call it going home whole," I replied. "Are you Cath-olic?"

He said, "Born one. But I haven't . . . you know how it is. I think I would've made a good medicine man."

He chuckled and I chuckled.

It was good, being able to talk it out.

I recommend talk as an antidote for a broken heart. Bob Alvarez and I talked the night away. But I still went back to Malibu with my heart in pieces.

I had, after all, sent my love home without me.

Alvarez wrote the draft of his official report closing the Sloane case at Pointe House that night. There was no sense asking for trouble, and certainly he would have been in a lot of trouble trying to document his experiences in that house, so he merely omitted all references to anyone but me. Actually there was no need for anything else. The sergeant had been withholding quite a bit of info from me. The Newport Beach police were holding a file of audio tapes from Hank Gibson's office—telephone records—it seems the guy recorded every call going across his desk. Those tapes revealed a conspiracy between Gibson and the younger Sloane going back for more than two years, even while the elder Sloane was still functional and controlling the Medici account—minor pilfering and manipulation of funds—apparently initially designed to allow young Sloane to have his cake and eat it too; that is, a way around the restrictive covenant: Jim Sloane and Hank Gibson were secretly in partnership and using the Medici money to fund their holding company.

Thieves often fall out though, and these two were no exception. While Jim Sloane was content to idle back and steal small, Gibson saw a way to walk away with the whole pie. He'd developed connections both in Sacramento and Santa Ana, and evidently he had managed to manipulate official records in both places, deleting crucial filings that established the Pointe property as an estate-in-trust and setting it up for takeover.

There remains much to be learned about all that, supposing someone were interested, but the whole question became moot for me when Valentinius walked away from it. It was my clear understanding that he desired no official fight over the property, and that is perfectly understandable under the circumstances; one official question always leads to ten or twelve more; I am sure he preferred to simply cut his losses and walk away.

There was no one left to quarrel with anyway.

Alvarez and I put it together that Jim Sloane must have looted the Medici file to back up Gibson's manipulations of the official records. Old Tom Sloane discovered the attempted fraud and couldn't handle it, if we are to take Valentinius at his murky truth. The knowledge drove old Tom up the wall, and his way of handling it was a total breakdown.

The death grimace I'll have to leave for your own understanding. I have told you what was told to me in that regard. Both Jim Sloane and Hank Gibson died officially of a heart attack. You can guess as well as I about the circumstances that produced those attacks in two healthy young men. The police do know that Jim Sloane visited Hank Gibson in Newport Beach early during the evening of both deaths. They think that Gibson was the first to die, but time of death is not usually as precise a matter for coroners as the public is led to believe.

Alvarez theorized that Gibson died while Sloane was with him. Sloane then drove to Laguna, left his car on Pacific Coast Highway and walked into the estate to avoid notice, and went to search my suite for information. He died in that search. Alvarez conveniently placed the heart attack on the little balcony just outside my bedroom; the body toppled over the low railing and plunged to the beach.

So much for neat police reports.

I tend to believe the murky truth from Valentinius. Angels do not kill I'm sure, but they can reveal truth—and sometimes, as Val suggested, the truth can kill. That is good enough for me.

I don't know what to tell you about Hai Tsu or her particular kingdom of heaven other than what you already know. Her collaboration with Valentinius could have been —and I suggest you consider this seriously—could have been a sort of joint effort. Like, you know, the U.S. and Soviets linking up in space as evidence of goodwill and international cooperation, etc. Clearly Hai Tsu was not under Val's direct authority; she served by some other charter, and please don't ask me to speculate on that—except to note that Jesus himself declared that in his father's house there are many mansions. I do not know which mansion Hai Tsu came from, but I daresay it is a very nice one.

I went back beneath that mountain a week later but had

to go in via the tidal cave; there was no longer a door in the cellar or elevator pit, but I could detect a faint outline in the stone where maybe a door had been. The passageway between the tidal cave and the smaller chamber was still intact, but the chamber itself was in ruins, as though some one or some thing had pulled a pin or something and undermined the whole structure. I found, yeah, some concave sections of rock that were very smooth on the inner surface, almost glasslike, but I found no stainless steel or whatever that stuff was.

I used that paper from Valentinius to tidy up behind him. Took all the money left in the Newport bank, nearly half a million, and divided it between the two ladies left behind without a job by the deaths of the Sloanes. I figured the long years of loyal service was deserving of that small reward; they could have a fling or two to brighten up their old age. I'm sure Valentinius approved. Old Ed James, the third partner in the firm, was apparently never involved in the Medici affair; he was Tom's brother-in-law and actually the only surviving relative. Technically anyway, the firm itself survived but James is living on borrowed time and will be going home one day soon.

My contact in Switzerland ran into a stone wall regarding the dealings there. He could ascertain only that money was finding its way in by various routes—and on the very day that he accessed the principal account, a freeze order had been imposed to lock up all funds until further notice, but he could not ascertain the source of that order. You wouldn't think that heaven needed currency, would you, but I guess you have to play any game under the rules where the game is being played. I kept my ten grand as part of the deal and figured I'd earned it; though it was small consolation for what I'd lost.

We can't count wins and losses in this kind of game though. As Val suggested, our infinity is large enough to contain them all, and all are headed inexorably toward the same point. "Error is perfection in process," yeah, I could buy that. Had to, 'cause I'd witnessed the process.

Funny thing about processes though. I went back to Malibu that morning—after the grand slam at Pointe House—a total wreck, almost completely out of it, feeling used and abused and very sorry for myself—smarting too over the idea that maybe I'd been playing a bit at the game of God and who the hell was I to be tinkering with people's lives that way?

As is my usual custom, I undressed en route from my back door to my bathroom, tossed the clothing in a pile, and stepped into the shower. I was in there I guess five minutes, just soaking up the hot water and ventilating suppressed rage and pain. First thing I noticed when I came out of that shower was the fact that the clothing I'd ejected en route to the bathroom was missing. It simply was not there. Remember, I had been wearing an outfit from the Pointe House wardrobe. I guess it was inviolate while it was on my person—but once I shucked it, it was off and running to wherever the other stuff went.

Next thing I noticed was a new decorative effect in my living room. A new painting occupied the wall space above the fireplace. It was titled *Soul Mates*. That painting still hangs there. You can come and take a look at it any time you'd like. It may startle and bedazzle you though, the same as everyone else who has seen it. Obviously a master work and straight from someone's heart.

That takes me back to where I started, doesn't it. It has been a difficult story to tell. I still do not fully understand all of it. And I still hurt a bit from it. But things got a lot better in that department during the week following the experience. I kept pretty busy, did a lot of shuttling between Malibu and Laguna tying up loose ends with Alvarez and seeing to several legal details concerning the property. The state has it now, by the way, and it looks like the developers won't get their hands on it after all. A move is underway to add the property to the parklands.

Anyway, I was telling you about the funny way things sometimes can process. I'd been staying busy. On the third night after Francesca went home, I dreamed very vividly of her. It was not a long dream; I just saw her in this strange place, performing strange tasks having somehow to do with the origins of art; it was not all that clear what she was doing—I just knew that she was supremely happy. And that dream gave me a new insight into the truth behind Francesca. Remember the Francesca I and II problem? I had thought that II was trying to take over I. Wrong. Francesca I was trying to assimilate Francesca II—and II was the one lying in that hospital bed at Irvine. I checked it out with her former roommates. It's true. The Francesca they knew was overbearing and demanding, often haughty and rude, very much a problem personality. They did not even go to her funeral. I did and saw her parents there. Nice people. I did not approach them, feeling that I could add nothing but confusion to their loss.

You're probably having trouble too with all that personality—assimilation bit. Who were the six other Francescas and why were they there? Why not all forty? I don't know either; I've been working on that. I think maybe the six were the strongest of the forty—not necessarily the most recent but the most highly developed—and that they had a strong stake in that process. I have heard mystics speak of these things, the working out of important problems in a state somewhat resembling the purgatory of the Catholics, and I have heard of resolution within the flesh—similar to the psychiatric resolutions within our own sphere.

You might work on this idea a bit yourself and let me know what you come up with.

For myself, I've come a long way since that night at Pointe House. I awoke from that vivid dream several nights later and went straight to my study to write down something that awakened with me. I will give that to you as an afterword here. It has meaning for me in dealing with the aftermath of Francesca; I leave it to you to decide what that meaning is.

I will close this account by again admitting that I do not know what reality is. I wish I did; but I can live okay without that knowledge for now. I know that I am real. Beyond that I know that something that is peculiarly me responds to something that is all around me. I feel that from that response flows experience, and that experience is tied in somehow to the reality that is existence itself. I know too that Francesca is real; not *was* real, *is* real. Hai Tsu and Valentinius and all the others are real; I know that they are because they help me define myself to myself, and because we are bound together in experience and by experience.

Soul mates?

Sure why not. Valentinius, that rascal, had known it all along, and he knew also that this experience would be her severest test. I was indeed the man for him.

Some day, some where, I would like to think that *he* will be the man for *me*. It is not impossible.

AFTERWORD

I believe that Francesca gave this to me after she'd gone home:

A Lovers' Creed

Because I love you,
I happily put you first in any issue involving
   personal comfort or desires;
I could not do otherwise,
And love you.
But in any issue involving personal conscience
   or sense of rightness and wrongness
      in conduct toward a third person,
         or some personal sense of duty,
The one thing that our love cannot endure

is for you to insist that I behave
    as though I were you
        instead of myself;
You cannot supplant me—nor I, you—
For we cannot love each other
    if we cannot be ourselves
        and respect ourselves—
Cannot even know that we are loved or loving,
    except as we know who we are—
And know that ultimately we stand before God
    naked and accountable
        for our own conscience
            and our decisions under that conscience.
I can love you only as myself,
    not as another;
I want you to love me only as yourself;
For no other love can have meaning
    for either of us,
And I cannot find that love or return it
    if I do not know who we are.

Thank you, Francesca. I really needed that.

Author's Note

The quotations on the life of St. Germain are taken from: *The Comte de St. Germain: The Secret of Kings* by I. Cooper-Oakley, originally published by Ars Regia of Milan in 1912 and republished by Theosophical Publishing House, Ltd., of London in 1927 and again in 1985. The volume is very much in print and available through any bookseller in the U.S. and Great Britain.

I recommend it to all as an interesting read.

—dp